P9-CQG-037

My Life as a Gamer

JANET TASHJIAN

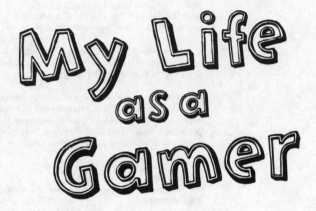

My Life
as a
Gamer

with cartoons by
JAKE TASHJIAN

SQUARE
FISH

Christy Ottaviano Books
Henry Holt and Company
New York

SQUARE
FISH

An imprint of Macmillan Publishing Group, LLC
175 Fifth Avenue, New York, NY 10010
mackids.com

Library of Congress Cataloging-in-Publication Data
Tashjian, Janet.
    My life as a gamer / by Janet Tashjian ; illustrated by
Jake Tashjian.
        pages   cm.—(The my life series)
    Summary: Derek Fallon gets the chance of a lifetime
when he is asked to test software for new video games,
but he soon discovers that his dream job isn't all it's
cracked up to be.
    ISBN 978-1-250-14368-6 (paperback)
    ISBN 978-0-8050-9865-5 (ebook)
    1. Children's art. [1. Video games—Fiction. 2. Tutors and
tutoring—Fiction. 3. Middle schools—Fiction.
4. Schools—Fiction. 5. Family life—California—Los
Angeles—Fiction. 6. Los Angeles (Calif.)—Fiction.
7. Children's art.] I. Tashjian, Jake, 1994– illustrator.
II. Title.
PZ7.T211135Mycm 2015   [Fic]—dc23   2014039906

Originally published in the United States by Christy
Ottaviano Books/Henry Holt and Company
First Square Fish edition, 2018
Square Fish logo designed by Filomena Tuosto

10 9 8

AR: 5.3 / LEXILE: 850L

For Christy Ottaviano—
our fifteenth

My Life as a Gamer

An Offer
I Can't Refuse

Here's the thing no one tells you about monkeys: They steal your cereal every chance they get. Lucky Charms, Cocoa Puffs, Froot Loops, Trix, Gorilla Munch—even the boring ones like Grape-Nuts—drive my capuchin monkey, Frank, out of his mind. He's like a castaway finally on dry land who can't wait to eat everything in sight. I hate keeping

castaway

nuggets

measure

him locked in his cage while I eat in front of him every morning, but on the days I let him out, the kitchen ends up looking like a rainbow war zone with flakes and nuggets all over the floor. My mutt, Bodi, is much more well behaved, waiting patiently for me to measure out his food and place it in his bowl near the bookcase.

"How about some chocolate chip pancakes?" my dad asks.

I say yes, mainly so I can take Frank out of his cage. (Frank is not a fan of pancakes.)

My dad hasn't worked for the last two months, so he's on kitchen patrol. He's been a freelance story-board artist for decades, but the movie industry's in a slump and it's been hard for him to find new work. Luckily, my mom's a vet, so they've

still been able to pay the bills. The
good news is my father has started
experimenting with some great new
recipes. The bad news is he's taken
an even greater interest in my
homework.

experimenting

Since I was little, the best way
for me to learn my vocabulary words
was to draw them. I have notebooks
and notebooks and notebooks filled
with illustrations of stick figures
acting out all my school words. My
parents have always inspected my
work, but these days Dad puts each
drawing under a microscope.

inspected

microscope

"Are you sure that's the best
definition of *inquire*?" He traces my
illustration with his finger.

"Shouldn't we add more chocolate
chips to the batter?" I ask, changing
the subject.

My dad throws another handful

of chips into the bowl. "If you want to continue with your art, you have to get every detail right. Believe me, I know."

reflect

Now I wish I'd just had cereal. Sweeping up Cap'n Crunch is ten times better than listening to Dad reflect on his old jobs. I hope he gets a new one soon—I'll miss the pancakes but not the sad stories.

"Hey, I forgot to tell you," Dad says. "I got an email from one of the guys at Global Games, where I did some work last year. He asked if I knew any kids who might be interested in testing some new software." He gently places three pancakes on my plate.

"Are they looking for kids to test video games?" I shout.

My dad pours himself a second

cup of coffee. "Does that mean you're interested?"

I don't even bother with the maple syrup, just roll the pancakes into a log, yell good-bye to my dad, and race to school to share the news with my friends.

WE'RE GOING TO TEST VIDEO GAMES!

My Friends Go Nuts

expectation

The mention of taking part in a video game study makes Matt ricochet off the walls with expectation. He's talking so loud and fast that Ms. Miller sticks her head out of the classroom to tell him to be quiet. Matt lowers his voice but is still excited.

"They want us to test video games before they're released? We'll probably be locked in a secret room and have to sign a form that says we'll keep everything confidential." He's whisper-shouting so close to my face, I can smell his peppermint toothpaste. "Wait until Umberto hears about this. Carly too."

"Hears about what?"

Matt and I whip around to see Carly standing behind us. She's wearing her T-shirt from surf camp with a hyena riding a giant wave. Matt gestures for me to tell Carly the news, and I do. As soon as I finish, Umberto screeches over in his wheelchair, so I repeat the story one more time.

I don't know about my friends, but I can barely concentrate on schoolwork for the rest of the day. (Not that I'm good at staying on task

confidential

peppermint

hyena

the rest of the time.) Ms. McCoddle leads a spirited debate about the American Revolution, but I listen to only every other word. What if we get to help name the new video game? Will we be listed in the credits?

"What do *you* think, Derek?"

When I wake from my daydream, Ms. McCoddle is standing beside my desk.

"Um...the people in Boston wanted coffee instead of tea?"

I pray my answer ties in somehow to what the class has been talking about, but by the look on Ms. McCoddle's face, it doesn't. She crosses her arms in front of her chest. With her black-and-white-striped shirt, she looks like an unhappy referee.

referee

"No, Derek. Paul Revere was a silversmith. But maybe he liked to hang out at his local Starbucks to get some of that coffee you mentioned." Several of my classmates laugh, so Ms. McCoddle keeps going. "Do you think Paul Revere was an espresso kind of guy, or do you think he preferred Frappuccinos?"

silversmith

All I want is for my teacher to walk back to her desk, but of course she doesn't.

Matt chimes in to bail me out. "Paul Revere definitely needed caffeine to make that midnight ride."

caffeine

Umberto shakes his head because I got caught not paying attention yet again. Carly laughs as Matt

spiel

continues his "the British are coming" spiel.

Ms. McCoddle arches her eyebrow and finally moves on, which is great because I want to get back to thinking about new video games.

Here She Comes to Wreck the Day

All my mother wants to talk about is the house call she made this afternoon to take care of two sick peacocks. In her vet practice, she usually doesn't get to work with exotic pets, so when she has a chance to examine a bobcat or a lemur, she grabs it.

I want to talk about Global Games but my mother's acting like someone on one of those hoarding shows, except what she's hoarding is the conversation.

dreamily

"They actually keep peacocks on the farm to calm the horses. Maybe it's the color or the plumage, but it seems to work." She looks dreamily out the kitchen window. "They're such a beautiful blue."

It seems like my whole life is spent listening to grown-ups drone on about stuff I'm not interested in.

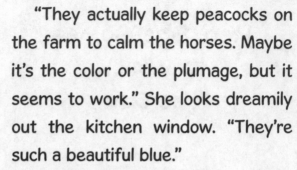

babbling

On the scale in my mind, I try to decide which topic is worse: Paul Revere or peacocks. As my mother continues babbling, I picture Paul Revere riding through the streets of Boston on a peacock, warning people about the British. Bodi must be bored with my mom's conversation too, because he snuggles alongside my leg underneath the table.

Just as I'm about to interrupt my mom's story, she switches subjects. "Dad says it's time for a new reading tutor, and I think he's right."

"Then I guess you guys should get one," I answer.

"Very funny," she says. "But I believe he was talking about you."

When you add them all up, I've had more reading tutors than babysitters. On one boring afternoon last year I made a list and rated them from #1 (Kimberly, who looked like a runway model) to #12 (Mrs. Gainesville, who smelled like moth-balls and mildew). The thought of adding yet another tutor to the list makes me want to bludgeon myself with the mallet my mother uses to pound chicken breasts. I'm about to loudly protest when she shows me a picture on her phone.

runway

bludgeon

"Her name is Hannah. She is majoring in political science at UCLA and coaches several kids your age in reading. She has very good references."

I look at the photo, not focusing on the girl's smile or black glasses, but on her Pac-Man T-shirt. It's a nice transition to tell my mom about the video game opportunity.

transition

"That's great," she says. "Do you think your friends can join you?"

I tell her I hope so because they're already counting on it.

"Sounds like fun—after you meet Hannah and get started on your reading."

Where's that mallet?

The Details

To say I bug my dad about calling his colleague at Global Games is an understatement. First I ask him every ten minutes, then I text him every five. When he stops answering me, I know I have to get more creative, so I use my markers and make a banner that reads, WE ARE READY TO TEST VIDEO GAMES. When that doesn't work, I take the batteries out of all the remotes, knowing Dad will open the junk drawer to get new ones. A long paper accordion falls out of the junk drawer that says, PLEEEEEEAAAAAASSSEE!!!!!!! I'm kind of surprised that ploy didn't work, so I write on the windshield of his car with soap. Unfortunately, I use my mother's special eczema soap that you can only get with a prescription. Double unfortunately, each bar of soap costs forty-eight dollars. It's difficult figuring out which parent is angrier. As they face me down, I decide it's a tie for first place.

prescription

"I'm not sure video game testing is in your future," my mom begins.

My father tosses me a large sponge. "I'll tell you what IS in your future—washing my car."

Frank gets the sponge before I

do and starts tossing it into the air. I yank it out of his hands before he tries to eat it.

"Being in the focus group will help with all kinds of skills," I plead, realizing a new way out of my dilemma. "There'll be so much READING—reading manuals, reading instructions. It'll be like having months of tutoring for free." This last part is an appeal to my mother, who's the biggest bargain hunter I know. I've seen her pull the car over several lanes of traffic when she spotted her favorite clogs on sale for half price.

I bite my tongue and wait for their decision. My mother and father look at each other, then my mother lets out a long sigh. "You can apply for the video game testing—if and

plead

dilemma

bargain

only if you focus on your reading too."

I start to leave but my father blocks me at the door.

"The bucket's in the garage," he says. "And don't forget the sponge."

I try to sneak Frank outside to "help," but my mother already has him back in his cage. It would be more fun to wash the car with a monkey but I can't complain.

Video games, here I come!

Umberto Is the Ringer

My friends bug me ten times more than I nagged my dad to get details on the focus group. When I finally have the info to share, I'm both happy and relieved.

nagged

"My dad's friend says the session starts this Saturday, from ten to three."

"I'm going to rule this game!" Matt seems awfully confident,

confident

especially since we don't know who else will be there.

Carly shakes her head. "You forget how good I was at FarmVille," she says. "You couldn't even figure out how to grow crops."

Now it's Umberto's time to disagree. "I've been designing apps for the past year in that after-school computer class. I know how these programmers think."

trounce

It suddenly dawns on me that the three friends I've invited to join me could trounce me with their gaming skills. For a brief moment, I get the urge to call the whole thing off but realize I'll be tarred and feathered if I do. I have to get used to the fact that I'll probably be at the bottom of the pack. Again.

"Hey, Derek," Matt says. "Don't

you think it's funny they want you and me in a FOCUS group?"

I'd feel bad he was making fun of me if what he was saying wasn't 100 percent true.

I hold out my hand for Umberto's phone and ask to see the new app he just finished. The four of us spent hours playing his first one, a really fun bowling game. This new app features a samurai warrior with a saber, slicing pepperoni with lightning speed and flinging the slices onto pizza dough, all the time avoiding dastardly cheese graters.

saber

dastardly

"You're really good at this," I tell Umberto as I swipe my finger across the touch screen. "Maybe you'll end up getting a job at Global Games someday."

Matt agrees, but Carly's already

onto the next thing, going through the papers in her folder. (They're organized and color coded, of course.)

"The state tests are in a few weeks," she says. "We're really going to have to study."

Matt, Umberto, and I stare at her blankly. We're talking about video games, and she's bringing up state tests?

"I'm not kidding," she continues. "Those tests are serious business."

"Don't be such a bummer," Matt says. "We're testing video games on Saturday!"

Carly shoves the papers into her pack. As she heads to class, she shoots me a look from the corner of her eye, and I know she brought up the state tests because of me. Carly's always been concerned about my reading disability. She's tried to help me study in the past, but our tutoring sessions usually end in mutual frustration. I hate to admit it, but I've been worried about the state tests since Ms. McCoddle told us about them a couple of weeks ago. (Yes, I *do* pay attention sometimes.) Maybe my parents are right and it IS time for another reading tutor, as long as she doesn't take any time away from my top priority—testing video games.

mutual

I'm a Little Worried About Dad

splattered

When I get home from school, I'm shocked to find a drop cloth, buckets, and rollers all over the kitchen floor. Half the kitchen walls are covered with new wallpaper featuring blue sea horses and bubbles. My father's T-shirt and jeans are splattered in wallpaper paste.

"Um...does Mom know about this?" I ask.

"It's a surprise," Dad answers. "She always hated these boring beige walls."

I point to one of the sea horses, whose head and tail are not lined up. "I think this is bathroom wallpaper."

"Of course it is," Dad says. "But you know how your mother loves the unpredictable."

Mom may enjoy the unpredictable when it comes to wearing wacky shoes and healing peacocks, but I don't know how she's going to feel about staring at uneven sea horses while making lasagna.

lasagna

"How's the job hunt going?" I ask.

My dad slathers a sheet of wallpaper with paste. "Really great. Lots of leads to follow up on."

slathers

My mom walks in, carrying three bags of groceries. A long baguette

baguette

nibbling

sticks out of one of the bags, almost jabbing her in the mouth, and I wonder how she got from the car to here without nibbling on it. She looks around the messy kitchen, then smiles kindly at my dad.

"Jeremy, how fun!"

My father holds out his arms, showing off the room. "It'll look great once I clean everything up." He wipes his hands on his jeans and goes out to get the rest of the groceries. Before I can say anything, my mother runs her hand along the crooked seam of the wallpaper.

seam

"Sea horses in the kitchen? Your father's got to get a job soon."

For once, my mom and I are in complete agreement.

Mom unpacks the groceries and tells me that Hannah is on her way over for our first tutoring session.

"But we didn't even interview her yet!"

"I interviewed her while you were at school," Mom says. "She's very qualified." Mom puts several bags of pasta in the cupboard. "If you don't like her, we can talk about getting someone else."

qualified

My usual tactic would be to argue, but I'm hoping this tutor might be one of the good ones. I know you're not supposed to judge a book by its cover, but no one said anything about judging people by their T-shirts. Not to mention the fact that I need all the help I can get if I'm going to pass those state tests.

My father resumes his wallpapering; my mother gives encouragement, but then hurries to her office next door so she doesn't have to witness the crazy mess that is now our kitchen.

I ask Dad if I can take Frank out of his cage, but both he and I know that's inviting trouble while the room's in such disarray. Instead, I let Bodi out of the den and grab a slice of leftover turkey and head to the backyard. I've got an hour till the new tutor comes, so I settle into my favorite spot near the jasmine against the fence to partake in my favorite activity.

Sitting with my dog, doing nothing.

disarray

partake

Tutor #13

The young woman on the front steps extends her hand. "My name is Hannah Yee, but you can call me Hannah Banana."

"Do I have to?"

She laughs. "The last student I tutored called me that."

"Was he three years old?"

She laughs again, too loud for the quality of my joke. "No. She was

suspenders

sixteen and aced her SATs. You should be so lucky."

Hannah is the only person I've ever seen in real life wearing suspenders, but her sneakers are custom pro skateboard shoes, so she looks cool. I realize I might actually be out of my league.

"Whoa! Who's that?" Hannah's face fills with delight when she spots Frank, and she bulldozes past me to get to his cage in the kitchen.

I explain that we're Frank's foster family and he's living with us until he goes to Monkey College. Before she can ask me what Monkey College is, I tell her Frank comes from an organization in Boston that trains capuchin monkeys to help the disabled.

She looks at me with mistrust. "You're kidding, right?"

Hannah isn't the first person who doesn't believe Frank's skills. I take him out of his cage and bring him to the living room.

mistrust

"DVD," I tell him.

Frank obediently scampers to the DVD player and presses the button that opens the tray.

Hannah covers her mouth with her hands, surprised at Frank's dexterity.

dexterity

"Watch this." I turn to Frank. "IN."

Frank takes a DVD from the stack and inserts it into the player.

Hannah looks confused. "I thought you said he'd learn this in Monkey College. How come he already knows how to do it?"

I take pride in my answer. "I

figure since he's with us anyway, he might as well learn stuff." It dawns on me that some of my classmates probably think this way all the time—trying to get ahead in their schoolwork instead of falling behind like me. Why am I teaching my monkey better study skills than I have?

Hannah makes me show her every trick Frank knows, which includes unscrewing the top to a water bottle and turning the light switch on and off. The fun—as always—is interrupted by my mother.

"Are you two getting ready to work?" She's wearing scrubs, so I know it's a day she'll be in surgery.

Hannah assures my mom she's brought a ton of work for us to do and she can't wait to get started.

Upon hearing the word *ton*, I tiptoe toward the back door with Frank. My vigilant mother grabs me by the elbow and puts Frank back in his cage while Hannah spreads out a stack of papers on the table.

vigilant

"This is going to be *fun*," Hannah says. As if to emphasize the point, she claps her hands.

Great—now I'M the trained monkey.

Saturday Is Finally Here

I get up early so I can hang out with Frank before my mother starts in with her rules and regulations. It means I'm the one who has to change Frank's diaper, but he's so happy to see me, I don't mind. I take Bodi outside to relieve himself, but he gets distracted by a squirrel, and we end up outside for twenty minutes. When we get back to the kitchen, my father's making break-fast burritos with scrambled eggs, black beans, and rice. He seems saddened when I douse his master-piece with ketchup.

saddened

Since he hasn't been working, Dad's got a bit of a beard going, which I can tell my mom isn't crazy about. But the only thing that matters today is that he's driving my friends and me to Global Games. The focus group is being held at one of the movie studios, and by the time we reach Culver City, Umberto's pulling up with Bill in his specialized wheelchair van. There's so much anticipation in the parking lot, I think my dad's SUV might explode with nervous energy.

douse

specialized

Before he leaves, my dad turns to us with his Serious Father Face.

"Ask for Tom when you get inside. And it goes without saying, you all need to behave—I know these guys."

My friends and I quickly agree to be on our best behavior.

I've been on this studio lot before, but my friends haven't. Carly's mouth hangs open as we walk by the soundstage where they film *Jeopardy!*

soundstage

"Whoa!" It's not one of the famous TV shows that has Umberto in disbelief; it's the giant line outside the building we're headed toward. He lets out a long whistle. "I thought there'd be only a few kids here today."

Carly does a quick scan and decides there are almost fifty kids in front of us. "Suppose we don't get picked?"

Matt tells her not to worry, that my father probably took care of everything. But maybe my father's name doesn't mean as much at Global Games as Matt thinks it does and we won't even make the first cut. This could be like one of those reality shows where contestants get voted off before the competition even starts. I tell myself not to fret, but I do.

competition

Matt takes the lead and goes to the front of the line to ask if Tom's around. A guy with an official Global Games lanyard tells him Tom's inside and gives Matt handouts for us to read while we're in line. Instead, we entertain ourselves by making up stories about the people in front of us.

fret

lanyard

"See those three guys in the

matching Wreck-It Ralph T-shirts?"
Umberto asks. "They're triplets
from Germany who moved to
Hollywood to make it big. They talk
in silly character voices the whole
time they play."

"That girl with the pigtails and
the X-Men backpack doesn't want
to be here," I chime in. "Her parents
make her play video games as
punishment when she doesn't clean
her room."

"The guy with the gold space
helmet is the number one Play-
Station player on the planet," Carly
says.

The three of us race to correct
her.

"The number one PlayStation
player on the planet is El Cid," I say.
"No one knows what he looks like."

Carly points to a photo in the brochure Matt gave us. (She, of course, was the only one to even look at it.) "That *is* El Cid. Global Games flew him here for the focus group."

Matt and I jump on the back of Umberto's wheelchair to get a better look. Nobody knows El Cid's identity; he apparently wants to keep it that way by hiding inside his golden space helmet, cape, and gloves.

identity

"Every gamer knows El Cid," Umberto says. "If he's here, we don't have a chance."

"Maybe they want to test kids with regular skills too," I suggest. "They can't just make games for super-geniuses."

"If El Cid's a super-genius, then she's obviously a girl," Carly says.

"She COULD be, but she's not," Umberto says. "El Cid's a twenty-year-old guy from Peru who got into MIT when he was seventeen. The rest is a mystery."

The line inches forward until we finally reach the large metal door leading to the Promised Land. We give the guy our names, and he checks us off without a lot of fanfare. I guess it was silly to think we'd get special treatment just because my dad did storyboards for a few video games last year.

fanfare

But another guy with a Global Games baseball cap proves me wrong. (Not that THAT'S hard to do.) "You're Jeremy's son!" He introduces himself as Tom and goes on and on about what an amazing artist my father is. "And he's so *funny*," Tom gushes. "Last time he was here, he had us all on the floor. Literally, on the floor, screaming with laughter."

I'd describe my dad as mildly funny, certainly not the comedian Tom makes him out to be. Matt starts sucking up to Tom by joining in on how hilarious my father is. I try not to roll my eyes at Matt's obvious attempt to brownnose one of the guys running the event. When I look over at Carly, she's smiling. One thing about Carly—nothing gets by her.

hilarious

Umberto wheels over to tell El Cid he's a giant fan, but the best he gets out of the gaming whiz is a nod. While he's doing that, Matt and I pretend we're magicians by making four doughnuts disappear in less than a minute. From across the

inhaling

room, Carly shoots us a mom face telling us to stop inhaling the free food, so I grab a napkin and focus on Tom, who's trying to quiet everyone down.

He looks around, then pulls a whistle out of his pocket and blows it really loud. "Let the games begin!"

A Quiz?!

Tom divides us into groups of three, which means one of us has to join another group. Umberto, Matt, and I stare down Carly, who gives us the evil eye before heading to the center of the room.

"Do you think she feels like we ganged up on her?" I ask.

"No more than any other time," Matt answers.

summon

Umberto can barely summon the strength to speak. "Look whose group Carly's in!"

We turn around to see Carly smiling like the cat who ate the canary as she takes a seat next to El Cid.

"That could have been me," Umberto says.

"Or me," Matt adds.

advantage

"Maybe that's what we get for ditching her." I can't help feeling a pang of guilt for the way we sometimes take advantage of Carly's good nature.

"Maybe she'll get some tips," Umberto says in a hopeful voice.

An intern passes out giant handbooks to each table. The manuals are thicker than the Los Angeles Yellow Pages my mom insists on keeping even though we never use them. "Are we supposed to READ this?" I ask.

A guy at the next table with a lame bandana tied around his neck looks at me and sneers. "No, this is an origami workshop. Start ripping and folding!"

origami

Everyone at his table laughs, and I can feel my cheeks flush.

"That WAS kind of funny," Matt admits.

I'm grateful when Tom continues. "You lucky people will be the first kids in the universe to play our new video game." He pulls off the black cloth covering the monitor in the front of the room. "Say hello to Arctic Ninja!"

universe

Everyone in the room lets out a giant "OOOOHHHHHHHHH!"

screenshots

habitat

"If the rest of the graphics are anything like this, this game will be huge!" Umberto says.

Sure enough—the screenshots that cover the board are filled with intricate details of exotic landscapes and lush colors. I've played a lot of video games that take place in different settings, but the incredible habitat of this video world is unlike anything I've ever seen.

"So first, everybody go through your manual. Then after you take the quiz at the back of the book, you'll be ready to play!"

"Did he just say QUIZ?" I whisper to Matt. "No one said anything about a quiz!"

"On a Saturday!" he adds.

But as I look around the room, everyone else has already started reading. Some kids are turning pages so fast, I wonder if there's a wind machine nearby. Umberto's on page six before I even get through the first paragraph.

For some reason I thought being part of this focus group would be a break from reading, a place where I didn't feel ten steps behind everybody else. Maybe I could even be BETTER at something than most kids for a change. It's becoming clear that I should get used to being at the lowest rung of the ladder— not just in school but also in life.

Even though she's at the next table, Carly's mind-reading skills are in top form. When I look over at her, she's staring at me with her Are-You-Okay? face. I appreciate her constant support—I just wish I didn't always need it.

constant

I do what I always do when I have

a big reading assignment—skim ahead to see how many excruciating pages I have to look forward to. Ninety-seven?! In my case, it looks like the light at the end of the tunnel is a train.

hunker

"There's no way around it," Umberto says encouragingly. "Better get started if you want to play."

He's right, of course. I hunker down and begin.

A few hours later I look up at the clock and realize that only ten minutes have gone by.

It's going to be a long day.

Carly
Surprises Us

When we finally break for lunch, I'm horrified to discover my friends are already cleared to move on to the video game room. I pretend I am too, not admitting I still have fifty pages to go. (Yes, I kept track of each page like a New Year's Eve countdown.)

admitting

We heap our plates with macaroni and cheese, salad, and chicken

countdown

refill

wings, then refill our lemonade glasses several times. I am heading to the table with the others when Tom calls me aside.

"It looks like you're having a tough time with that reading," Tom says.

I didn't know my reading disability was something physical like a broken leg you could see from the outside.

"No worries," Tom continues. "I'm sure you've read enough to join the rest of the group."

I thank Tom, but inside I think, *If the reading wasn't so important, why did we have to do it in the first place?* I realize getting angry would be a waste of time and decide just to be grateful for the reprieve.

reprieve

When I join my friends, they're all staring at the table near the door.

"El Cid has to eat sometime,"

Umberto says. "We're waiting for him to take off his helmet."

We're not the only ones checking out the gaming legend; most of the other kids in the cafeteria are watching El Cid too. The whole room sighs when El Cid stands up, grabs his tray, and heads out of the room.

"He's probably going to eat in one of the conference rooms," Matt suggests between chicken wings. "Or maybe one of the bathroom stalls."

conference

Carly covers Matt's now gigantic pile of bones with a napkin so she doesn't have to look at the debris of all those chickens. "The company made one of the private dining rooms available," she says. "They want to help El Cid maintain his privacy."

debris

privacy

It's strange for Carly to be the one with the inside scoop—she hardly ever played video games until she started hanging out with us.

"Don't act like you're El Cid's new best friend," I tell her. "You probably didn't even talk to him."

She gives me one of her sweetest smiles and holds up her cell. "Then why did he just text me?"

"WHAT?!" Umberto, Matt, and I grab for the phone, but Carly jumps up from the table and reads the incoming text.

incoming

"El Cid says the macaroni and cheese tastes like paste." She types a response while the three of us look on in astonishment. "It could use some bacon," she reads as she types. "Bacon makes everything better."

astonishment

I ask Matt and Umberto why Carly is always ten steps ahead of us.

Matt looks at me like I have a python slithering out of my ear. "Duh, because she's a girl. They always kick our butts. Get used to it."

slithering

"Everybody finished?" Tom shouts a bit later from the front of the room. "Your new Global Games video awaits!"

We empty our trays into the trash and head toward the double doors. It's been three hours since we got here, and my fingers are itching to finally get hold of a controller.

controller

The room is gigantic, filled with long rows of tables. Every table has ten seats and high-end monitors, each with its own console. If Christmas, Hanukkah, Halloween, summer vacation, and my birthday were suddenly transformed into a room, it would look exactly like this.

"I never want to go home," Matt says.

"I'm bringing my sleeping bag next weekend," Umberto says. "They're going to have to drag me out of here."

photographs

Carly takes a few pictures with her phone until an intern races over and tells her we're not allowed to take photographs. Carly's never in trouble, so it's fun to see her reaction the few times she is. "I was just going to show Mrs. Kimball at the media center this cool room design." Carly flushes. "It's not like I'm spying on their precious video game."

"Maybe you can unmask your new boyfriend El Cid too," I suggest.

"He's not my boyfriend!"

unmask

"Are you sure?" Umberto points to the other side of the room, where El Cid is motioning to Carly. She walks away in a huff to join the gaming legend, leaving the three of us nobodies in the dust.

What I CAN Say

The good news is: Arctic Ninja is the most amazing game my friends and I have ever played. It's THAT good.

The bad news is: We can't tell anybody.

Don't try to get details out of me, because I can't say a thing, except to my dad, who ended up talking to Tom about Arctic Ninja this week.

"What's your favorite part of the

game?" Dad asks me on the drive to the hardware store. (His new project is replacing all the doorknobs.)

"It's hard to pick just one part," I answer.

He makes me tell him what I know about the game so far.

narwhal

"Well, there's a narwhal called Skippy that knows martial arts. He has to swim through fourteen different levels while being bombarded by razor-sharp icicles being shot from a flying drone. If you make it through the booby-trapped igloo, you discover a portal leading to different worlds. While under constant attack, you need to find the secret code and break it before the lemmings do. Not to mention there's a bloodthirsty snowman who pops up unexpectedly.

bombarded

portal

bloodthirsty

And don't forget a narwhal's horn is treasured by poachers, so there's plenty of THEM around too. Plus, the background music has a million hooks and you'll NEVER get it out of your head."

My father smiles. "And that's just Level One."

Talking about Arctic Ninja makes up for the fact that it takes Dad forty-five minutes to pick out doorknobs.

That's right. Doorknobs.

Why Is Saturday Always So Far Away?

As a normal twelve-year-old, I spend most of my time desperately waiting for the weekend, counting off each school day, each chore, each homework assignment until Saturday finally—FINALLY—arrives. But since I joined the video game group, it's like the entire world's in slow motion, dragging out each minute of school so long that I want to scream. The fact that the state tests are coming up only makes things worse.

"We're going to be spending a lot of time preparing for these tests. But I'm sure all of you will do well."

paranoid

I admit I can be completely paranoid when it comes to tests, but it does seem like Ms. McCoddle might be focusing today's little speech on me.

"It pays to be prepared," she continues. "That means some things might have to take a backseat—things like sports, music lessons, skateboarding, texting, video games. These things may all *seem* important—"

"Because they ARE," Matt interrupts.

"But so are these tests." Ms.

McCoddle gives Matt's desk a little rap with her knuckles as if that somehow gives her the last word.

"She was TOTALLY talking to me," I tell Carly after class.

"You're not the only kid who skateboards and plays video games. Besides, you don't take music lessons; I do." Carly suddenly seems worried. "Do you think Ms. McCoddle was talking about ME?"

"All I know is that these tests are NOT getting in the way of Arctic Ninja."

scoots

Carly scoots in front of me to get my full attention. "I know how hard studying is for you, but you're really going to have to buckle down."

"You sound like my mother. Cut it out!" I look around for Matt and Umberto to save me from Carly's good intentions. Unfortunately my friends who AREN'T obsessed with schoolwork are nowhere to be found.

Carly finally lets me off the hook. "I can help you!" she calls down the hall.

Friend or no friend, the last thing I need is help from a smarty-pants like Carly.

My Kind of Studying

Umberto and Matt come over after school to strategize. Not about the state tests—DUH!—but about Arctic Ninja.

strategize

I feel bad for not inviting Carly, but after her nagging today, I think we might have more fun without her.

"Okay," Umberto starts. "If they brought El Cid to test this new game

similarities

observation

and El Cid is the top PlayStation player in the world, then maybe we should start with some PlayStation games in case there are similarities."

It's a good observation; I can tell Umberto's given this a lot of thought.

I pull out the controllers from the basket under the TV. It's almost as if turning on the television makes my mother magically appear.

"When you said you were working today, I thought you meant on homework," she says.

"We ARE," I lie. "But we're warming up with video games first. Like stretching before a run."

Mom seems amused. "Do you think playing video games will warm up your muscles for the language arts or math parts of the test?"

"Definitely math," Matt answers.

"There are so many studies about math skills improving when kids play video games."

My mom's almost laughing now. "I didn't realize you read a lot of scientific studies, Matt. I'd love to see some of them."

scientific

"I'll email them to Derek," Matt says. "I think you'll find them interesting."

I give my mother a You-Can-Go-Now face, but she sits on the edge of the couch in no hurry to leave. Where's a sick ferret in need of deworming when you need one?

"Let's see . . . the last study about video games I read had to do with childhood obesity." My mother has no intention of letting the subject drop. "In fact, I even read an article about a boy who sat in the same

obesity

embolism

position for so long playing video games that he died of an embolism."

"MOM! Stop trying to scare us! We're not going to die playing video games."

After I beg my mother fifty times to leave, she finally does. It takes Umberto, Matt, and me several minutes on the Internet to find out that an embolism is a blood clot.

"If I haven't gotten one in this wheelchair, I probably won't get one playing video games," Umberto says.

I assure him no one's getting any blood clots today.

"Well, your mom certainly threw a wet blanket on any kind of fun," Matt says. "Maybe we SHOULD just study."

"The only thing we're studying for is kicking butt on Arctic Ninja. Agreed?"

"Agreed."

We play our favorite games for the next three hours. (I kill them both in Madden and FIFA, then get killed in Crash Bandicoot.)

superstitious

It might sound superstitious, but after my mom's comment, I make sure we get up and move every twenty minutes.

Just in case.

Someone Else
Wants to Play

buzzkill

clueless

My mom remains a buzzkill for most of the day, but after my friends leave, Dad sits next to me on the couch and picks up a controller to my Wii U.

"Is this Arctic Ninja?" he asks.

Poor Dad, so clueless in the world of video games. I explain that of COURSE Global Games won't let us take the new game home; it's a top secret prototype that can't leave the building.

ROBOT PANTS TESTING

prototype

"I was KIDDING," he says. "I know how much these companies guard their new products. So which game is this?" He points to the graphics on the TV.

"It's the new Mario Kart game I'm going to annihilate you in." I set the game for two players and hit PLAY.

It takes some time for Dad to get the hang of it, but after a while, he actually makes a pretty good opponent.

"So, we're trying to keep winning races and collecting shells, right?" My dad's beard is patchy, and he's still wearing his sweatpants from working out this morning. It's almost as if he's resigned himself to being

resigned

home all day. His wallpapering and baking activities have tapered off, and I'm not sure if that's good or bad.

"I may not be able to beat you," Dad says. "But at least let me beat the computer."

I've been trying to get Dad to play video games with me for years, and I can count the times he has on one hand. So spending the next hour beating him in Mario feels pretty great. We only stop playing when Mom drags us away for dinner.

Dad tousles my hair as I put the controllers away. "You beat me fair and square. I'm just glad I didn't come in eighth. But I still want a rematch."

I tell him, "Anytime."

The first piece of bad news for

the evening is that we're having scallops for dinner. The second piece of bad news is that Hannah's coming over for another tutoring session.

scallops

"Why didn't you tell me?" I complain. "I need to mentally prepare if I'm going to work all night."

My mother rolls her eyes, a skill she's mastered while living with me. "You played video games all afternoon," she says. "I doubt a few hours of studying will kill you."

If I were the kind of kid who was good at research, here's where I'd quote some depressing statistic proving that too much studying CAN actually kill you. I'm sure there are examples of some poor kid who got buried alive under a stack of text-books during an earthquake or

depressing

another unlucky student whose brain exploded from one too many long division problems. Unfortunately, my reading skills aren't good enough for me to track down this valuable information in a timely manner.

Before I finish moving the scallops around my plate, Hannah's at the back door. Mom asks if she'd like some dinner, but Hannah says she's eager to get to work. I tell her I can't THINK about studying until I've cleared the table and done the dishes.

Both my parents almost choke on their salad. My dad composes himself and pulls his phone from his back pocket. "Would you mind repeating that sentence so I can record it? It'll be fun to play it back when I need a good laugh."

"Come on, Derek," Hannah says. "Time's a-wastin'."

It may just be my imagination, but when I feed Bodi some of my scallops, he seems to look at me with pity. I begrudgingly follow Hannah into the den.

imagination

Too Many Notes

taskmaster

sergeant

Hannah seems like she might be all right to do normal things with, but she's a taskmaster when it comes to tutoring. It's hard to believe that someone wearing flip-flops, a Sonic the Hedgehog T-shirt, and purple stripes in her hair can act like such a drill sergeant, but that's exactly what Hannah is. I haven't seen so much of my own handwriting since

Matt and I spent a month obsessed with making cootie catchers.

"Are we almost done?" I ask for the zillionth time.

perky

We've been working for an hour, but Hannah still seems perky and ready to go. "Just a few more sections," she answers.

I remember how much Hannah loved Frank on her first visit, so I take him out of his cage to hopefully distract her. Before I can give her the rules of handling a monkey, she scoops Frank up in her arms. I take him back and explain how she needs to act around a capuchin. She listens closely, as if she might start taking notes. When I finally let her hold Frank, she seems happier than a two-year-old sitting on Santa's lap.

"So I guess we're done for

waltzes

tonight?" I pack up my notes before she can answer. This was certainly one of my better plans.

Hannah waltzes around the den, dancing with Frank and her own inner music. While she enjoys herself with my monkey, I stash all my schoolwork under the couch, then hit the kitchen for some snacks.

When I come back with a plate of Oreos, Hannah's still wearing her goofy smile, but Frank is gone.

"Where's Frank?" I look behind the curtain, one of his favorite hiding places.

scampered

"He scampered under the couch. I think he wants to play hide-and-seek." She bends down to look underneath the sofa, but I tell her to move slowly so that she doesn't startle him. Hannah gets down on

startle

her hands and knees behind the coffee table. "He's just lying there chewing on paper. It's adorable!"

I hurry next to her on the floor and slide my hand underneath the couch to bring out Frank. My worst fear has materialized—Frank is devouring my notes.

materialized

I whisk him onto the couch and try to salvage what I can of tonight's work. It doesn't help when Hannah starts laughing.

"Instead of the dog ate my homework, it's the *monkey* ate my homework. Funny, right?"

"HILARIOUS." I weed through the stack of mangled papers, but none of the pages can be saved. "I leave the room to get cookies and you let a monkey eat my notes? What kind of a tutor ARE you?"

mangled

Hannah's face changes from giggly to angry in two seconds flat. "You're the one who knows the monkey rules, not me. How was I supposed to know he'd eat paper?" She grabs her jacket and heads to the kitchen. I pick up Frank and race behind her, making sure my mom hears both sides of the story.

As a vet, Mom's first concern is for Frank. She checks him out to make sure there's nothing caught in his throat, then puts him back in his cage. If she was going to yell at me for taking Frank out or leaving loose papers around, she changes her mind when she sees my face. It's been a long time since I cried—and I'm NOT going to now—but I can't hide how frustrated I am. Mom gathers me in for a hug and tells me

I did a good job taking all those notes and she'll help me catch up tomorrow. She holds me until I get embarrassed and wriggle away.

Hannah apologizes profusely as my mother writes her a check and schedules another session for next week. I gather up the shreds of paper and bury them in the wastebasket under the remains of the stupid scallops.

For a brief moment tonight, I felt ahead of the game, as if defeating a test was almost possible. It's probably how Carly and Umberto feel all the time, but for me the feeling was certainly new. I should've known that kind of positive feeling about schoolwork wasn't meant for a second-rate student like me.

defeating

Saturday!

My dad and I get stuck behind a three-car accident on our way to the studio that sends me into an I'm-going-to-miss-everything state of anxiety. But we're native Angelenos, so we always leave early to drive anywhere. Even after sitting in traffic without moving for twenty minutes, I still make it to Global Games on time.

My friends are already in their groups; Carly's in a corner with El Cid, playing a game on his phone. I try not to feel resentful that Carly's the one hanging out with the gaming genius, but maybe she'll get some tips we all can use to raise our scores in Arctic Ninja.

resentful

Tom blows his whistle to get the day started. "Now that everyone's familiar with the rules, today's all about competition. Whoever gets the highest score by the end of the day wins a hundred-dollar prize."

The room buzzes with excitement. A hundred dollars!

Matt rubs his hands together as if winning is actually a possibility. Out of our group, Umberto's the one I'd bet my money on, but with El Cid here, I doubt anybody has a fighting chance.

Even though we're still in our groups, Tom tells us we'll be playing the game on our own this time. We spread out in the giant room, each kid with a twenty-one-inch monitor, console, and controller. It doesn't take long before the room erupts with the sounds of electronic lightning bolts, power surges, and explosions—not to mention shouting. As I move to the next level, I catch a glimpse of El Cid, calmly manipulating his controls. I'd give anything to know what his score is.

My own score continues to climb. I'm actually better at this prototype than I am at any of my games back home. Arctic Ninja seems pretty straightforward, even though the graphics are complex. All I can do is try my best and stop worrying about

surges

where I stack up against everyone else.

Later, when Tom blows his whistle for us to stop, I realize two hours have gone by. I look over to Matt, who gives me a thumbs-up. Maybe he DOES have a chance of winning the grand prize.

"Each console is matched to a number on the main system, so we have immediate access to your scores." Tom runs through screens on his iPad as he talks. "In third place, with 10,290 points, is the person at console 17."

immediate

Everyone hurries to find the number on the side of the console. The kid who made the crack about this being an origami class waves his arms in the air. Turns out his name is Toby. He makes a real fuss about coming in third, standing on his chair and pumping his fists in the air.

"Second place, with 11,782 points, is the person at console 6."

Umberto lets out a "Yahoo!" for everyone in the room to hear. I knew Umberto was good—he almost always beats Matt and me—but I had no idea he'd stack up this well against players from around the world. I swell with pride for my friend.

"And at 107,028 points, the player at console 8."

El Cid slowly gets up from his console and takes a bow to thunderous applause.

thunderous

"Come and get your prize!" Tom waves a crisp hundred-dollar bill in the air.

"He got more than a hundred

thousand points," Matt whispers. "That's insane!"

"I wonder if the helmet helps," I say. "Maybe I'll start wearing a disguise too."

"Yeah, like that Lone Ranger mask you wore all through kindergarten," Matt jokes. "It's like you thought school was one big masquerade party."

masquerade

As much as I try to keep a straight face, I can't help but smile. It's nice having a friend who's known you forever and can remind you of every stupid thing you've ever done in your life.

Carly comes racing over. "I got 10,120 points. Do you think I came in fourth?"

I check out Matt's monitor. He scored over ten thousand points too. Then I look at my own, with a meager

meager

score of 8,276. I'm really going to have to improve my gaming skills if I don't want to be the worst player in the focus group.

"Since we're starting the next game with these high scores, our numbers this afternoon should be gigantic," Umberto says.

"What are you talking about?" I ask. "Doesn't the next game start fresh?"

exchange

My three friends exchange glances as if my question doesn't make any sense.

"You saved your game, right?" Carly asked.

Matt looks down at the floor. "The manual said to always save your game when the session ends."

I look at my monitor. My score now reads a bright yellow ZERO.

"You didn't read that page?" Carly asks softly.

I close my eyes to think, but I can't remember if I read that important information and forgot or if I never read it at all. What I DO know is that I'm now thousands of points behind every other player in the room.

Tom announces it's time for lunch, so we follow the interns to the cafeteria. It's a giant buffet of ribs and french fries, but no amount of tasty food can make me feel better about today's screwup.

buffet

"I was right behind El Cid!" Umberto says between chews. "Second place, behind a pro!"

"Technically, you weren't RIGHT behind him," Matt says. "But second place is amazing."

I try to focus on feeling happy for Umberto instead of worrying about myself, now in last place. I look around the room at the large group of happy kids and wonder why it's so hard for me to be one of them.

It Gets Better

As I trudge back to my console to start Level One of Arctic Ninja all over again, I wonder if signing up for this focus group was a good idea. I mean, why am I feeling like a loser? It's a Saturday! I could be skateboarding, or hanging out at the Promenade, or eating pizza in front of the TV with Bodi and Frank. If I wanted to feel miserable about

trudge

promenade

myself, I might as well have just gone to school.

Tom tells us that in this round, the top THREE players will win prizes. I know I don't have a shot but am happy to race through the levels much faster than I went through them the first time. It's almost as if coming up from behind gives me a kind of video game superpower. My counter zooms past ten thousand points in no time. I don't know how the other participants are doing, because I'm using every bit of energy to lock into the world of Skippy the narwhal and his magic portals. But it's not my usual panic-stricken concentration; it's a relaxed kind of focus that for a moment makes me feel like I AM El Cid.

When I hear Tom's whistle, I hit

participants

the SAVE button immediately. I may not be the brightest kid in the room, but I'm not making the same mistake twice.

"With a score of 21,723, third place goes to the player at console 6!" Tom shouts.

Umberto pops a wheelie, then skids to a halt in front of Tom to collect his prize.

"He's gotten really good," Matt whispers. "I think all that programming's paid off."

"And in second place, with a score of 27,556, the player at console 4!"

My jaw drops to the floor when Carly strolls over to collect her winnings.

"How did THAT happen?" Matt asks. "It's one thing to beat US, but to beat Umberto?!"

paltry

Carly holds up the fifty-dollar bill and does a little happy dance on her way back to her seat. I look at my counter reading 19,876, a number that suddenly seems paltry compared to my friends'.

"And with an incredible score of 240,807 . . . "

Everyone in the room gasps at that outrageous number. Tom calms us down before continuing.

"First prize goes to the player at console 8."

El Cid strides to the front of the room as if winning two hundred dollars on a Saturday afternoon is no big deal.

loathe

"I'm beginning to loathe him," Matt whispers.

Umberto nudges Matt with his elbow. "Come on! You've got to give the kid some credit."

As we grab our things to go, Carly jumps up and down like a cheerleader. "I know exactly what I'm going to do with this money," she says.

"Never mind that," I say. "How'd you score so many points?"

"Yeah," Matt adds. "Is El Cid coaching you on the side?"

Carly stares us down. "Oh right! I'm not smart enough to figure out this game on my own?"

"No one's saying that." Umberto wheels over to Carly's side. "It's just that maybe you have some tips to share."

Carly still looks annoyed. "I might have gotten a few tips, but you guys should read the manual. Everything you need to know is in there." She hurries to catch up to El Cid, her new best friend.

"Reading a manual to get good at

a video game?" I say. "That's the stupidest thing I've ever heard."

"Come on," Umberto says. "Let's hit the snack table before we head home."

As we load up our pockets with granola bars, I'm genuinely happy for Umberto and Carly. And wowed by the talent of El Cid.

Couch Potato

Matt's brother, Jamie, is twenty minutes late picking us up, but we don't complain, because he's got a bag of steaming fish tacos waiting for us. By the time we reach my house, all that's left is a crumpled paper bag and empty salsa containers, which litter the floor of Jamie's car.

litter

I'm feeling warm and full when I enter my house and am shocked to hear the springing sound of Mario coming from the den. My dad's still in his pajamas in front of the TV.

"You're on World Eight?" I ask. "How long have you been playing?"

He waits until Mario dies before he answers. "Pretty much since breakfast."

I look at the clock on the mantel. It's almost four in the afternoon. "Um . . . where's Mom?"

He tells me she went shopping with a friend in Malibu and will be home soon.

"Then maybe you should get dressed?" It's weird to be the one giving advice about how to avoid getting in trouble with Mom.

"Just a few more minutes." He's staring at the screen so closely, I suddenly wonder if my mother was right about the whole Get-Up-And-Move thing.

"I was going to take Bodi for a walk," I suggest. "Want to come?"

This time Dad doesn't answer, just continues to stare at the screen. I'm actually happy when Mom's car pulls into the driveway.

"Dad, Mom's here. Want me to put this away?" I reach for the controller, but Dad yanks it away before I can grab it.

"I beat Bowser, so I get a secret world," he says. "Just another five minutes."

My mom comes into the house, carrying two fancy bags with ribbon handles, which means I'm probably not the recipient of her shopping excursion. She looks over to Dad, then to me.

recipient

excursion

"Don't tell me he's been at it all day," she whispers.

I tell her I found him like this when I got back from Global Games.

"He needs to find a job," we whisper in unison.

My father suddenly screams as if Bodi just got hit by a car.

shushes

"Jeremy!" my mom shushes. "Inside voice!"

I do a spit-take with my soda. I LOVE not being the one getting in trouble for a change.

"I almost saved the princess!" Dad complains.

Usually it's MY fun that Mom pulls the plug on, so it's crazy to watch her take charge with Dad. As she holds out her hand for the controller and shuts off the TV, Dad lets out a groan louder than one of mine.

Amusing as this scenario is, it's also unsettling. Is this what happens to grown-ups when they don't have jobs? Does Mom have to worry about both of us now? I'm happy to have someone else in the house who enjoys Donkey Kong as much as I do, but Dad DOES seem to be acting a little nuts.

unsettling

Yikes! I'm starting to sound like Mom.

Who Knew I Could
Keep a Secret?

Hannah goes totally bonkers when she hears about the Saturday focus group.

"El Cid is there? Are you kidding?" She proceeds to ask me two dozen questions about El Cid's identity.

inquiries

I answer her inquiries with a grin as if I have inside information, which of course I don't. Even though I've been in the same room with the gaming star for two weeks, I don't have a clue as to his identity.

Hannah persists, making me divulge every detail, which takes about two seconds, since all I can tell her is that El Cid wins every competition.

divulge

"Who knows," I say. "Maybe he cheats."

Hannah scoffs at the suggestion. "El Cid doesn't need to cheat—he *thinks* like a video game. That's why he's the number one player in the world. He's from Peru, you know."

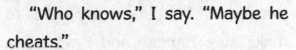

scoffs

I try to appear cooler than I am by saying El Cid's been hanging out with Carly, who happens to be one of my best friends. "They text each other all the time," I offer. I can't figure out if I'm trying to impress Hannah because she's a cool fangirl

fangirl

or because I want to distract her from the practice test she's supposed to give me today. Maybe a little bit of both.

My mom walks through the den with a basket of folded clothes. Sure, she COULD just be doing laundry, but I bet she really wants to make sure Hannah and I get down to business. Whether that's her intention or not, it does the trick; Hannah immediately slides the test across the table.

"This should give us an idea of how you'll do on the real tests next month." Hannah's talking to me but looking toward the kitchen, making sure my mother can hear. "They take forty-five minutes, so that's what I'll give you now. Go!"

peruse

I grab a pencil and peruse the

test. "Hey! I thought we were doing science today!"

Hannah shrugs as if an English test is interchangeable with any other kind of test.

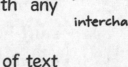
interchangeable

I point to the large block of text filling two pages. "I can't read all this!"

"You're in middle school. Of course you can."

Her lack of compassion makes me cringe. "I won't be able to read this and answer all these questions in forty-five minutes. I need more time!"

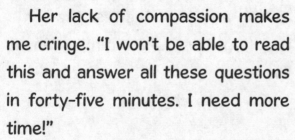
compassion

She pulls the gum out of her mouth in one long strand and tells me to chill. "It's just practice. No one cares."

"I care! If I flunk, I'm dead meat!"

Hannah holds up her cell and

points to the time. "Forty-three minutes left. Let's go!"

I stare at the two pages—TWO!—full of sentence after sentence of stuff I don't care about. I feel like a

mountaineer

mountaineer standing at the base of Mount Everest. You might be able to climb it, but you also know how much work it'll take to get there. I grab my mental rope, harness, and ice axe and start the test the same way you WOULD climb Mount Everest.

One step at a time.

Maybe I Shouldn't Head to the Mountains Just Yet

After forty-five minutes of blood, sweat, and tears, I only score a fifty-six on the practice test. Forget planting my flag at the summit of Mount Everest—I never even left base camp.

summit

My mom scrunches her face when Hannah shows her my results. She's not angry; she knows how hard I try—how hard I've been

scrunches

trying my whole life. She digs down and shoots me a small smile. "Next time will be better—I'm sure of it."

That makes one of us.

It Only Gets Worse

I've known Ms. McCoddle since kindergarten, but I've never seen her as stressed as she is today.

stressed

"We've been working on these practice tests for weeks," she says. "Today we'll see how we rank against some other classes."

She hands a stack of tests to the students in the first row, who pass them back. After this week's epic fail with Hannah, I'm not confident my skills will help our class in the rankings.

"Ms. Lynch and I have a bet," Ms. McCoddle says. "I said our class will leave hers in the dust. What do you guys say?"

A few kids let out some half-hearted grunts. I guess I'm not the only one worried about performing.

reminder

Ms. McCoddle says we have forty-five minutes to complete the test, and she'll give us a reminder along the way to let us know how much time has gone by. I take it as a good sign that the first essay is about Harry Houdini. Even though the level is harder than what I'm used to, I do like reading about Houdini's elaborate escape routines. There are only two questions at the end of all that reading; I make my best guesses and move on to the next section.

The next assignment is about a Greek god named Phaëthon, except there are two dots over the *e*, which COMPLETELY throws me off. Why can't they just use a regular *e*? How am I supposed to pronounce this, never mind read it? More important, how am I supposed to get through ten(!) paragraphs with all these dots hijacking my attention? I look over at Carly, who seems unfazed by the dots and all this READING.

pronounce

hijacking

unfazed

The last essay is about Koko the Gorilla. The story is interesting (I watched a TV special on Koko last year) but it makes me realize that Frank will be leaving us soon. Sure, we might be able to see him again but once he's in Monkey College and gets assigned to be someone's

assigned

companion, we probably won't. Then THAT person will be Frank's constant friend—not me. It makes me want to hide Frank at Matt's house and pretend I don't know where he is when they finally come to take him back to Boston. For some reason, I can't imagine my mom signing off on such a plan.

Ms. McCoddle claps her hands the way she used to when we had her for kindergarten. "Okay . . . stop!"

"WHAT?!"

Ms. McCoddle smiles as she collects our booklets. "Not enough time, Derek?"

How do I explain that there's NEVER enough time—to pass a test, figure out why letters need dots, or save your monkey from leaving.

At Least It's
Saturday Again

It comes as no surprise to find out I flunked the practice test. What IS surprising is that three other kids in my class did too. Turns out Ms. Lynch's class kicked our butts big-time, and Ms. McCoddle is not a happy camper. Our class spends every waking minute for the rest of the week going over the material again. So by the time Saturday rolls around, I'm more than ready to take out my frustrations in the world of Arctic Ninja.

There's always someone who complains about everything, and sure enough, the kid in front of me at the snack table is telling anybody who'll listen how lame Arctic Ninja is.

"There should be more worlds. And there definitely aren't enough Easter eggs." He spoons so much cream cheese onto his plate that he completely buries his bagel.

"I'm telling you, this game will be a giant flop—worse than Atari's E.T. They're going to end up burying all the unsold games in New Mexico— mark my words."

I don't want this guy's negativity to leak onto me, so I forgo one more doughnut and head to my seat.

forgo

Tom spends the first half of the morning asking us what kind of expansion packs we usually buy. After way too much group debate, he finally announces it's time to play.

expansion

"We're doing something different today," he adds. "We want to see how the group does with collaborative game play."

debate

Some kids seem excited; others disappointed. My gaming skills are less than average, so as far as I'm concerned, I'll take all the help I can get.

Before anyone gets a chance to choose a teammate, Tom races through his iPad, calling out names and dividing us into pairs. I listen for my friends' names too. Umberto and Matt are assigned to kids I

dividing

don't know, and Carly is teamed up with me.

Umberto motions to a really tall kid waving his arms in the air. "That lucky dog got El Cid for a teammate. Can you imagine? I bet he clocks the highest score of his life."

In front of everyone in the room, the goofy kid bows to El Cid as if he's the king of England. El Cid seems mortified and grabs the kid by the arm, bringing him back to an upright position. The tall kid still can't contain himself, jumping around like he's on an out-of-control pogo stick.

upright

"What a dope," Matt says.

"Are you kidding? That's exactly what I'd be doing if I was El Cid's teammate." Umberto spins around in his wheelchair. "If I could jump, that is."

Matt and I laugh despite ourselves; Umberto really is one of the funniest kids we know.

Carly comes over, rubbing her hands together as if she just found a secret map to buried treasure. "Let's do this, Derek!"

It's funny to see Carly so excited about video games after all the grief she's given us for the hours we've logged behind various controllers since we've been friends. But Carly's eagerness is catchy, and I find myself thinking she and I might actually have a chance at making the list of today's winners.

Because we're playing in teams, the game now moves faster and there are more obstacles to overcome. But I'm surprised to see how good Carly's gotten. She tosses

harpoon

me a harpoon when the man-eating snowmen attack and boosts me over the wall of ice blocks to avoid getting nailed by the icicle-shooting drones. I find myself saying "Nice!" several times at Carly's moves.

The fourth level of Arctic Ninja is my favorite part of the game. It's unpredictable, fast, and the graphics are incredible. So I'm surprised when an entirely different level unfolds this time. I guess playing collaboratively unlocks new scenarios. Other kids must've reached the new level too because the next thing I hear is a lot of people yelling "Whoa!" from across the room.

This new phase is visually unlike the rest of the game, so for a minute I'm disoriented and my narwhal kind of stands there, wondering

disoriented

what to do next—until Carly rams me out of the way of a demonic poacher.

demonic

"You totally saved me."

"More than once." She doesn't take her eyes off the screen.

Maybe it's because we're friends, but Carly and I find a rhythm that we use to our advantage for the rest of the game. When her narwhal moves left, I cover her so we don't get attacked by one of the poacher's evil minions. As soon as my narwhal reaches the toboggan to go to the next level, Carly jumps in front of me, throwing an extra narwhal tusk at the lemmings trying to get to the secret code before we do. Carly and I are unstoppable—at least in the virtual world of Arctic Ninja.

minions

toboggan

"We're still nowhere close to

finding the secret code," I say. "Where do you think it is? And why are letters of the alphabet flying by?"

"You're the animal expert," Carly says. "What are those fish our narwhals keep eating?"

"Arctic cod." There are so few times I know something Carly doesn't know that I try to savor the moment.

"That's where the flying letters come in!" Carly whispers. "Grab an E!"

It takes me a minute to figure out what she's talking about. The girl is a GENIUS. I wait for the letters to come around again and stab an E with my narwhal's tusk. Carly's grinning from ear to ear as I feed the letter to one of the fish.

"If you add an e to cod, you get

code," she whispers. "Do you think that's it?"

We both watch the screen as the fish swallows the bouncing vowel. Sure enough, a cutscene appears, depicting another layer of Skippy's story.

AEIOU(Y)
vowel

"I never would've gotten to this new level without you," I tell Carly.

"Ditto," she says. "But YOU'RE the one who knew that fish was an Arctic cod."

Tom suddenly whistles that the session is over.

"We make a good team," Carly says as she saves the game.

"It's weird, but we do." I want to change the subject before the conversation gets awkward. "I wonder how your buddy El Cid made out with HIS teammate."

awkward

I motion to the tall guy, who's literally dancing around the table, and then to El Cid, who looks uncomfortable.

"The results are in!" Tom waves his arms in the air to get our attention. "In third place, the team at console 3."

Toby the origami guy and a girl who looks much too young to be in this focus group walk to the front of the room to collect their prize.

"In second place, the team at console 7." The crowd goes dead-quiet when El Cid and pogo boy get up to claim their prize.

Umberto cranes in his wheelchair to see. "El Cid hasn't lost a game in three years!"

"He didn't LOSE," Matt says. "He came in second. That's different."

El Cid doesn't seem as surprised as the rest of us; he accepts his second-place prize with no fuss. Pogo Boy, on the other hand, goes MENTAL, as if Tom is handing him the Nobel Prize for Video Gaming.

"And first prize goes to the team at console 9!"

It takes me a second to realize that console 9 is US! I try to act cool as I walk to the front of the room, not like some luckless misfit who never wins anything—which is, of course, my true identity.

misfit

My cool act dissipates when Matt starts chanting "DER-EK! DER-EK! CAR-LY! CAR-LY!" until everyone chants along. I roll my eyes at the attention, but inside I love every minute of it.

It's the second time Carly's won a

prize, so she makes a real show of it, holding her fist in the air like she's now the poster child for a new Girl Power movement. Her buddy El Cid gives Carly a small bow when Tom hands us our prize.

A hundred dollars each!

"You just did the impossible!" Umberto says as we file out for lunch. "You outscored the number one player in the world!"

I can't take the credit; there's no way I ever would've racked up such a high score if it weren't for Carly, who's now surrounded by several other girls who want to congratulate her.

After a week of failing everything, it feels good to WIN for a change.

DER–EK!

DER–EK!

outscored

Bragging Rights

I rub my victory in Matt's and Umberto's faces whenever I get the chance, which is probably half a million times. I also spend thirty dollars of my winnings on new comic books. (Mom drives me to Meltdown on Sunset on the condition that I put the rest of the money in my savings account.) Most of the week is business as usual, until I get to

I'm better than you.

brag

brag about my win to Hannah when she comes over for our study session.

Hannah seems shocked. "YOU beat El Cid?"

How did she just make me feel like a loser for winning? "Yes, ME. I'm not a failure at everything."

"Give me the details," she says. "Don't leave anything out."

To prove that I actually AM good at something, I tell her how Carly and I made a great team during the cooperative play.

"Oh, so someone helped you," she says.

I now despise Tutor #13.

To make Hannah believe me, I share the details of our victory— from the multiplying ice block walls to our strategy for escaping the

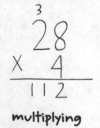

$$\begin{array}{r} \overset{3}{2}8 \\ \times\ \ 4 \\ \hline 112 \end{array}$$

multiplying

deadly icicles. I tell her about the narwhals, the killer snowmen, and the secret code until I feel like I've earned her respect.

respect

"Sounds like Carly's a good player."

I tell her she's never even met Carly.

Hannah starts going through her bag for the practice tests. "But I feel like I know her; you talk about her all the time."

I blush, wondering if that's true.

"Enough about your game," Hannah says. "It's time to do some math!"

I look at the clock on the kitchen wall. It seems like my entire life is spent sitting with work in front of me while I stare at clocks waiting for time to move faster.

"Go!" Hannah shouts with so much enthusiasm, you'd think I was in a skateboard competition instead of taking a stupid practice test. (Isn't a practice test still just a test? Does it make it any less terrible to call it *practice*?)

stalling

I stop stalling and begin the first problem. After a few minutes, I look up and see Hannah rapidly texting on her phone. She's probably a decade older than I am, but I gather my courage to question her anyway.

"You're not writing down any of that information I just told you about Arctic Ninja, are you?"

boredom

She puts down her cell and looks at me with an expression of sheer boredom. "I'm texting my roommate to meet me at the Grove tonight. Is that okay with you?" She points to the clock. "Come on!"

"I know, I know. Time's a-wastin'."

I settle into my work, and when Hannah grades me afterward, I'm thrilled to find out I passed my first practice test. It feels as if I'm riding the victory over El Cid like a giant wave all the way to shore.

The Wrong Kind
of Party

unveiled

unfamiliar

The people who come to Mom's veterinary office usually park on one of the side streets, so I'm surprised when I come home from school and find several cars in the driveway.

The mystery's unveiled when I discover Dad and some friends playing video games in the living room. I hang back in the doorway to take in this unfamiliar scene.

I recognize Dad's college friend Eric, and Mr. Jensen, who used to work with Dad a few years ago. I have no idea who the other guy is. The four of them are huddled around the TV, screaming at the monitor. Two empty pizza boxes and several beer cans litter the floor.

huddled

The kitchen clock reads ten after three. I only hope my mother has a full day of appointments and doesn't pop into the house to change clothes or grab a file.

"Hey, guys!" I shout in my happiest voice. "Who's winning?"

No one reads faster than me.

"I am!" Eric responds, barely looking up. "Your dad was ahead till he got too cocky."

cocky

"I was ahead till you cheated," my father yells back. "Derek, introduce yourself to Mr. Chapman."

The guy I don't know holds out his hand. I tell him it's nice to meet him and ask how he knows my dad.

"We met at Stan's. Your father's quite the storyteller."

The thought of my normally hardworking father sitting at the counter of the local doughnut shop, telling stories to strangers, fills me with dismay. I've been to Stan's with Dad a million times—they have the best peanut butter and jelly doughnuts in the city—but we've never sat at the counter to chat with people we don't know. I'm suddenly worried my father will never work again and we'll be forced to live on the street. Mom would say I'm letting my imagination get the better of me and to STOP, but my mind goes into overdrive.

overdrive

roused

I'm roused from my scary

daydream by a shout marking the end of Borderlands. After all my fears, when my father gets up from the couch, he's just regular Dad.

"You want a snack?" he asks. "Eric brought over some pretzels and chips." He tosses me the bags, and several pretzels fall out. Bodi scarfs them down as soon as they hit the floor.

Since I was little, my mom's always made a big thing about me cleaning up after myself. I'd say I'm successful with that maybe half the time, but now I find myself scooping up napkins, plates, and pizza boxes with lightning speed so Dad doesn't get in trouble. I bury the beer cans deep in the recycling bin.

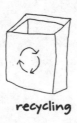

recycling

"We were playing Mario earlier," Mr. Jensen says. "Any tips so I don't get killed next time?"

protagonist

antagonist

ensemble

I tell him it's all about collecting the mushrooms and saving the princess, which leads to a lively discussion about the pros and cons of the Mario games. We debate whether Bowser makes a better protagonist or antagonist. (Mr. Chapman thinks Mario's better when he's part of an ensemble. No one else agrees, but he makes a forceful argument anyway.)

Even though I was apprehensive before, it's the most time I've spent with Dad and his friends, and I end up having a fun afternoon. Mr. Jensen wants to try a retro game, so we play a quick round of Space Invaders before he has to pick up his kids from their after-school program. Then Eric breaks into a whole routine about how sea horses don't belong on kitchen wallpaper.

Even though my dad's the butt of the joke, he laughs and I can see why so many people like hanging out with him. I know he wants a new job more than anything, but today he seems happy just to enjoy the company of his friends. Watching him goof around with Eric and Mr. Chapman reminds me of Matt, Umberto, and me sitting around the same kitchen table, bantering back and forth about stupid things too.

bantering

Maybe being a grown-up isn't so different from being a kid—just the same brain in a bigger body. I know I should be working on the practice test Ms. McCoddle gave us to take home, but for the moment I'm content to be talking about video games and wallpaper with Dad and my new grown-up friends.

You're Doing
What?

herd

I spent WAY too long hanging out with Dad yesterday and completely spaced on taking another practice test. I should've known Ms. McCoddle wouldn't forget; like all teachers, she has the memory of an elephant. Make that a herd of elephants. I barely have a chance to settle into my chair before she's handing out papers and pencils, barking out instructions for the next hour. I shake my head—is school ever going to get easier?

I try my best to answer the questions, but halfway through the test I come to the conclusion that I'm condemned to be at the bottom of my class—or any class, for that matter. I put my pencil down and lay my head on the desk.

conclusion

condemned

A few minutes later, I hear Ms. McCoddle's voice in my ear.

"You can *do* this," she whispers kindly. "I know you can."

I can't find the words to tell her I'm tired of trying, tired of failing, so I remain mute.

She picks up my pencil and makes it walk across the desk toward my hand.

"The Derek Fallon I know isn't a

quitter," she continues. "He doesn't give up."

I raise my head and look at Ms. McCoddle. She's one of the youngest teachers in the school, but she looks older since I first had her in kindergarten. I remember how nice she was to me when my mother used to drop me off for morning kindergarten and I'd sit by the window and cry. I always hated to see Mom go, but Ms. McCoddle would take me by the hand and lead me to the comfy loft with the picture books and pillows. Whether it's because she's looking at me with that same caring expression now or because I don't want my classmates to see our teacher hanging out at my desk, I take the pencil from her hand and sit up in my chair. The smile on Ms. McCoddle's face as I start working is almost worth the price of reading this boring essay on aqueducts.

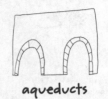
aqueducts

My positive feelings are short-lived when I realize I'll have to guess on the last fifteen questions if I'm going to finish the test on time. I pencil in the ovals and hope some of my random choices are correct.

The torturous morning is made a tiny bit better when the cafeteria ladies serve us enchiladas for lunch.

enchiladas

"That test was vicious," Matt says.

vicious

Umberto agrees. "Enough with the practice tests! Just give us the real ones and call it a day."

Carly pretends not to be

daintily

addressing me while she daintily cuts her enchilada. "I don't know if it's my imagination, but I think these practice tests are getting harder."

"As if any of these tests make *you* break a sweat," Matt says.

"That's not fair!" Carly snaps. "I studied for three hours last night."

Often lately, I find myself taking Carly's side. "Leave her alone," I tell Matt. "She can't help it if she's a brainiac."

"I'm NOT a brainiac," Carly says. "I work my butt off, and you know it!"

She picks up her stuff to move to another table, but I grab the edge of her tray and tell her to stay.

"What are you doing after school tomorrow?" I ask, trying to keep the peace.

She checks out the three of us to make sure we're not tricking her into staying. "I'm hanging out with a friend."

"We're your only friends," Matt teases. "So it must be one of us."

Carly takes the apple from her tray and hurls it at Matt, who catches it with one hand, then takes a giant bite.

"If you really want to know, I'm meeting El Cid," Carly answers.

It's as if someone's sprinkled quiet dust over the table because Matt, Umberto, and I are suddenly paralyzed.

paralyzed

"You're going to El Cid's house after school?" Umberto finally says.

"El Cid stays at a hotel every weekend, remember? We're meeting at the coffee shop."

"With or without his helmet?" Matt asks.

Carly smiles like the cat that ate the canary. "I'll never tell."

"We want to know everything!" Umberto practically shouts. "This isn't fair!"

"We aren't supposed to keep secrets from each other," I add. "You're not being a good friend."

"I AM being a good friend," Carly answers. "To El Cid. You don't want him to have to go into seclusion, do you?"

seclusion

Carly checks the time on her phone and says she needs to meet Maria before science class. The rest of us watch her head out of the cafeteria toward the double doors.

"She's passing us by," Matt says.

"They all do," Umberto adds.

"She's still our friend," I say. "She'll ALWAYS be our friend."

Even as I say it, I hope more than anything that it's true.

WHAT?!

badgering

I spend the entire drive to Culver City on Saturday badgering Carly about El Cid's secret identity.

"Did he take his helmet off last night?" I ask. "At least you can tell me THAT!"

Her smile can only be described as sly. "I'm not talking."

"He did!" I shout. "I can tell because you're grinning."

She gives my arm a little punch. "You can stop asking because I'm not going to tell you a thing." But she can't wipe the smile off her face.

"Come on," I beg. "Tell me SOMETHING."

"Let's just say we had so much fun I stayed for dinner."

"So he DID take his helmet off!" I act as if I've discovered some gigantic fact about El Cid, but in reality I still don't know anything about him. I bug Carly for the rest of the drive until she starts a conversation with my mother to shut me up.

I can tell from the moment we get to Global Games that something's wrong. The interns all look like someone stole their smartphones, Tom isn't wearing his usual smile, and the buffet of breakfast goodies is nowhere to be found. Carly heads over to her new best friend to see if he knows anything. Matt, Umberto, and I ask around to figure out what's going on, but no one's talking. We wait in stony silence until Tom hops onto one of the tables and addresses the group.

breach

"There's been a breach of confidentiality." Tom nods to one of the interns, who sends a screen-shot to the giant TV in front of the room.

Everyone gasps, but because I'm a slow reader, it takes me a while to figure out what everyone else is murmuring about.

"A person with the screen name PORT47 has posted most of the details of Arctic Ninja—the drones, the igloos, the lemmings, the secret code, the narwhals, everything." Tom takes off his baseball cap and rubs his head. (Until now I didn't realize he was bald.) "Does anyone know how this could have happened?"

Everyone in the group looks around the room wondering the same thing. Who could've DONE this?

rework

"We obviously need to rework the game, which is too bad," Tom continues. "We can't risk any more information leaking to our competitors, so we might have to cancel this focus group."

Several kids are visibly angry.

"That's not fair!" the pogo guy yells. "One bad apple shouldn't spoil it for everybody else."

"It also wasn't fair for somebody in this room to blab the details of the game on the Internet." Tom scans the room as if trying to X-ray our souls and find the guilty party. "We WILL find out who did this."

I'm listening to Tom but can't stop staring at the screen. The Web site that leaked Arctic Ninja looks familiar, and I can't figure out why...until I remember it's a gaming site I've seen Hannah use on her phone. I squint and read the post more closely. A growing sense of dread starts in my toes and spreads to the rest of my body when I realize the post contains all the aspects of the game I shared with Hannah when I was bragging about my win. No. No. No. This is NOT happening.

squint

"We'll get to the bottom of this," Tom repeats. "I promise you that."

Everyone in the room looks worried, but no one is more afraid than I am.

Why is everything always my fault?

Should I Come Clean?

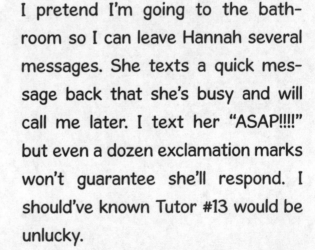

I pretend I'm going to the bathroom so I can leave Hannah several
messages. She texts a quick mes-
sage back that she's busy and will
call me later. I text her "ASAP!!!!"
but even a dozen exclamation marks
won't guarantee she'll respond. I
should've known Tutor #13 would be
unlucky.

unlucky

As we drive home, I stare out the

window and try to decide what to do. My friends complain about how unfair the whole incident is, but I keep my mouth shut, wondering whether I should tell them about Hannah.

On the one hand, my friends often have good advice—especially Carly. On the other hand, I'm embarrassed that my big mouth could've led to not only leaked corporate secrets but possibly the end of our super-fun Saturday focus group. Umberto, Matt, and Carly will have my head on a platter if they find out I'm the one who spilled the beans.

After we drop off my friends and get home, I decide to swallow my pride and come clean to my parents—which is easier said than done. I follow Mom from the laundry room to the kitchen to the garage before she finally stops in her tracks and asks what's going on. By the time I'm halfway through the story, my father's joined us. When he realizes I might have undermined the work of his colleagues, he is NOT happy.

undermined

"Let me get this straight," he says. "You agreed not to disclose any information about the new game, yet you told Hannah all about it?"

disclose

"She didn't believe I could win, so I told her how I did. I didn't think she'd leak it!"

My mother takes a deep breath and lowers her voice. "Were you bragging? Is that what happened?"

Leave it to my mother to quickly

get to the bottom of things. With a bit of shame, I admit I was.

I can almost see the wheels turning inside my father's brain as he paces around the driveway. "We don't know for sure that it was Hannah, so I don't think you should say anything just yet. Let's keep a lid on this for now."

My mother drops the basket of laundry with such force several socks fly onto the lawn. "Jeremy, you can't be serious. Even if it ends up NOT to be Hannah, Derek should tell them so they can rule her out."

"These are people I've worked with, remember? Let's not be impulsive and make their lives more difficult." My father tosses the socks back into the basket as if everything's decided. "I say we sit

impulsive

on this for a while and let the pros at Global Games figure it out."

I check my phone to see if Hannah's gotten back to me, but she hasn't. I apologize to my father for the tenth time before my mother cuts me short.

"You're not a little kid anymore, Derek. When you give your word, you should mean it—not throw your principles away to brag about a high score on a video game."

I know Mom's right, but her comment makes me angry. I snap my fingers for Bodi to follow me upstairs and spend the rest of the evening staring at my phone.

But Hannah doesn't call.

My Own Version
of Arctic Ninja

To say I'm worried about Hannah being the leak is an understatement. I text her a million times and even check the Web site that broke the story to look for clues. My parents argue about the best course of action, while I keep my head down and stay out of their way. So when Ms. Miller gives us some free time at the end of science class on Tuesday, it's a welcome relief.

understatement

scheme

monologue

Matt, Umberto, and I use the time to scheme different ways to win Arctic Ninja. Because I do most of my thinking with a marker in my hand, I sketch the different characters in my notebook as we talk.

After a ridiculous monologue about how he's going to beat El Cid, Matt crosses over to my desk and laughs when he sees my drawings. "Narwhals don't wear sombreros! That's the most ridiculous thing I've ever seen."

"Not any more ridiculous than a sponge living in a pineapple."

"Hey," Matt says. "You can call him Skippy Gonzales!"

Umberto digs a marker out of his pack and starts drawing too. When he first transferred to our class, we fought over who was the best cartoonist. Now our love of cartoons is something that unites us as friends.

unites

Matt flips through my notebook, enjoying several of my drawings: the snowman from Arctic Ninja gnawing on a rack of ribs; Calvin, Hobbes, and Skippy holding on to a toboggan for dear life as they leap across a snowy hill; and the icicle-wielding drones writing SURRENDER DOR-OTHY across the sky. Matt loves how crazy the drawings are so I take photos and text them to my dad.

gnawing

I look over to see if Ms. Miller cares that we're goofing around, but she's helping Andy with the periodic table, so I head to the front of the room to see what Carly's up to.

She doesn't hear me approach,

curlicue

and I'm shocked to see the doodles in the margin of the language arts notebook in front of her. I'd recognize Carly's curlicue handwriting anywhere, but I'm shocked to see the words she's written now.

Derek Fallon.

The sound of my eyes popping out of my head must startle her because Carly suddenly throws herself on the notebook as if she's trying to extinguish a fire.

"I always doodle. It helps me think," Carly says.

I'm glad Matt's on the other side of the room because he'd be TORTURING Carly right now. Carly's always so self-assured that it's strange to see her this flustered.

self-assured

flustered

"I doodle all kinds of things too," I say to make her feel better. "Look at my narwhal from Arctic Ninja."

Carly's so relieved I'm not focusing on my name in her notebook that she laughs much longer than a narwhal in a sombrero deserves to be laughed at. She makes me show her the rest of the illustrations before we head to our next class.

But just for the record: A girl doodled my name in her notebook!

Unexpected Fun

When I eventually swallow my pride and ask Carly to help me study later in the week, she tells me her cousin Amanda's in town from San Diego, but she's happy to study anyway. Here's a riddle: What's worse than studying with one girl? Answer: Studying with TWO.

I ride over to Carly's with as much enthusiasm as if I were biking to the dentist to have all my teeth pulled.

Her cousin Amanda is much taller than Carly; she even has a few inches on me. She's kind of shy and laughs nervously at every lame attempt I make at a joke.

"We're watching animal tricks on YouTube," Carly says. "Check out this Jack Russell terrier. He can do more things around the house than Frank."

terrier

The video is funny, and for a minute I get geared up for an afternoon of watching one cute animal caper after another, but I should know Carly better than that. After the video, she leads me to the dining room table, which is set up like a mini library with cups full of pencils, erasers, and stacks of paper. I tell

caper

Carly she didn't have to go to all this trouble.

"What are you talking about? This is how I normally do homework." Carly brushes away bits of eraser crumbs from the tabletop and offers me a seat.

"Don't worry," Amanda says. "We have the same tests at my school, and I'm afraid of taking them too."

Amanda now seems less like Carly's perfect cousin and a little more like me. I look at her closely. Her hair is darker than Carly's and really long, almost to her waist. She wears tiny pearl earrings as bright as her superwhite teeth.

employing

"My parents keep employing tutor after tutor, but I'm not sure they're doing any good," Amanda continues.

"That's how I feel!"

"I know they want to help, but it seems like such a waste of money."

"Not to mention time."

Carly points to the two of us. "Since you're both my friends, I figured studying together would be fun."

"I thought she was your cousin?"

"She's one of my best friends too, okay? And just so you know— neither one of you leaves till you do okay on the practice test."

Amanda shoots me a little smile when Carly turns away. I feel my cheeks flush; I hadn't expected to have so much in common with Carly's cousin. The afternoon shifts from a medieval torture chamber to almost fun—as long as Amanda doesn't beat me.

tyrant

But of course she does. (Neither of us did well, but her score was higher than mine.) Carly is a tyrant when it comes to practicing; she makes us take another test. After an hour, she finally lets us have a break for snacks.

As we munch on some home-made trail mix chock-full of chocolate chips and walnuts, Carly tells her cousin about my notebooks filled with vocabulary words.

"How many do you have?" Amanda asks.

"Notebooks or drawings?" I ask.

"Drawings."

I tell her too many to count but more than a thousand.

"You act like you're such a bad student," Carly says. "But look how many words you've learned over the years."

Amanda takes a low bow. "You, Derek, are the king of vocabulary words."

sensei

"The sensei of vocabulary words," Carly adds.

For a minute, I think they're goofing on me, then realize they're sincere.

"I guess I HAVE learned a lot of words," I say.

"Good! Then you can put them to use now." Carly quickly clears away the trail mix and brings back the paper and pencils.

I should've figured all this adulation was just a way to get me to focus on work. But I feel a bit better about studying, and I do okay on the next section. My mom texts that she and my dad are waiting so we can go to visit Mrs. Mitchell at her new home in Calabasas, so I say

adulation

good-bye. Carly and Amanda both seem a little sad to see me go.

On the drive to Calabasas, my mother gives me a pep talk about how all this studying will definitely pay off. I appreciate her positive thoughts but wonder if this is one of the rare times that she's wrong. I stare out the window at the cars whizzing by and hope she isn't.

The Day of Reckoning

Thanks to Mom, Saturday has gone from Fun Day to D-Day. She insists I tell Tom about Hannah and forces Dad to come with me to make sure I do. We drive to Global Games in silence, as if we're both on our way to the guillotine.

guillotine

"You know confidentiality is a big thing with corporations," he begins. "They spend billions of dollars developing these movies and video games, so they can't afford to have any leaks—especially in these days of social media where anybody can take a picture with a phone and post it online for the world to see."

I can tell this is only the tip of the lecture iceberg, so I interrupt him as soon as I can.

iceberg

"I only mentioned a handful of details about the game to Hannah. How was I to know she'd turn out to be a spy?"

I don't have the nerve to tell Dad that I finally heard from Hannah yesterday. It was a one-word text—SORRY!—as if any kind of apology could make up for the tsunami of trouble she left in her wake.

tsunami

When Dad and I find Tom inside, my father nudges me forward. I wait until Tom is done talking on the phone and then clear my throat.

"I think I have an idea who's responsible for leaking the details of Arctic Ninja," I say.

Tom looks at me but addresses my father. "Jeremy, I'm surprised Derek would be involved. You know how important it is to keep this stuff confidential."

My father gestures for me to continue. I tell Tom the sad tale of Hannah and the game.

"Derek," my father interrupts. "This isn't about Hannah; it's about you."

"I know I wasn't supposed to brag about the game to anyone. But HANNAH posted it on the Internet, not me! You can't blame me for that."

Tom listens intently, then thinks for a few seconds before answering, "We at Global Games take this kind of thing very seriously, so we had a team of people on it immediately. It didn't take our experts long to trace the posting back to the computer it came from."

I breathe a sigh of relief. "Good! Maybe you'll have better luck tracking Hannah down than I had. She sent me only one text and hasn't answered any of my calls."

"Actually," Tom begins, "it wasn't your friend Hannah. It was someone from the focus group...who's just been escorted off the premises."

I look around the room to see who's missing. After doing a mental head count, I realize the origami guy isn't here. "Was it Toby?"

"I guess he couldn't wait to brag about his score either," Tom says. "Unfortunately, he won't be playing Arctic Ninja anymore."

It slowly dawns on me that Hannah didn't do anything wrong after all. I turn to my dad, who doesn't look any happier with the news.

"You understand it was still wrong to divulge details of the game—even if Hannah *didn't* post them," he says.

I tell him I do, but inside all I'm thinking is I'M OFF THE HOOK—until Tom brings me back to reality.

"Just because your tutor wasn't the leak doesn't mean I'm not disappointed, Derek."

Tom waits for me to respond, but all I can do is say I'm sorry one more time.

"Apologizing is one thing," Tom continues, "but I hope you learned something. If you were over eighteen, there'd be legal consequences for a breach like this."

He and my father both look at me expectantly, and I finally get how big a deal this confidentiality thing really is. For the first time in my life, I don't want to be older; I'm happy just to be twelve.

When Dad pulls Tom aside for a private chat, I hurry through the room to find my friends. I might get another lecture on the drive home and I wish I hadn't disappointed Tom, but right now I have to contain myself from shouting.

I STILL GET TO PLAY ARCTIC NINJA!

An Unexpected Argument

It turns out the reason Hannah hadn't called is because her grandfather was rushed to the hospital. She had to drive through Death Valley and Joshua Tree to see him. She said it was such a desolate part of the state that she didn't have any reception and it was hard to get back to me. I know Mom thinks Hannah could've at least

desolate

taken a minute at the hospital to return one of my frantic calls, but because the state tests are next week, she told Hannah she was glad her grandfather was okay and scheduled her to come this week. I decide to spare Hannah the gruesome details of the Arctic Ninja leak and concentrate on math and language arts instead.

"I was so worried about my grandpa," Hannah says. "And all that driving! Hours of desert and those amazing trees. It was like being on Mars."

When I tell Hannah there are no trees on Mars, she hits the search engine on her phone faster than Frank can swipe a half-eaten sandwich off the counter. She holds up her phone with a photo. "See? There *are* trees on Mars."

I explain that the spikes in the photo might LOOK like trees, but they're actually plumes of carbon dioxide.

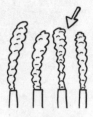

plumes

She speed-reads the article and tells me I'm wrong, that they ARE trees, which leads to a lively discussion about believing everything you read on the Internet. I tell Hannah we examined those same photographs in Ms. Miller's class last year and realized someone had posted the pictures with false claims on a bogus science site. It makes me happy to be smarter than a college student—at least in this particular instance. But I also think, *What a horrible tutor I have!*

bogus

I hadn't planned on it, but all this talk about Web sites leads me to tell Hannah about the Arctic Ninja scandal.

scandal

Hannah seems crushed when I tell her I thought she was the one who posted the details online. She eases herself slowly onto the kitchen chair. "Is that why you kept texting me a million times? I thought you were worried about your tests."

"I AM worried about my tests. And if you thought I was worried, why didn't you call me back?"

She stares at the coffee cup ring that my mom's tried to scrub out a million times but is permanently embedded in the tabletop. "You thought I leaked a secret? I'd never do that."

For a moment, I feel like Hannah might start crying, which comes close to throwing me into a full-blown panic attack. What am I supposed to do here? Apologize? Comfort her? Hide?

Just as quickly, Hannah's sadness turns to anger. "While I was visiting my grandfather, you were telling Global Games that I stole information? Did you give them my name?"

"No! At least I don't think so. I didn't hear back from you. What was I supposed to think?"

Hannah's attention is no longer fixed on the coffee stain but on me. "Derek, you are an immature boy who will *never* pass those tests."

Her venomous words strike me like one of the icicles in Arctic Ninja. "Why are you being so mean?" I ask. "I thought you leaked the information, but I was wrong. Don't insult me!"

"Does that mean I shouldn't make fun of you for reading like a

venomous

little kid too? Or imitate how you still have to run your finger under every sentence?"

I'm too dumbfounded to answer, but I don't have to.

"Pack up your things and go," my father tells Hannah. "That's not how we treat people in this house."

Hannah doesn't seem embarrassed by the fact that my father has suddenly appeared in the doorway. She glares at him with the same icy stare she uses on me.

"Good luck on your test, Derek. You'll need it." Hannah grabs her stuff and slams the door on her way out.

outburst

My father shakes his head sadly. "That outburst was completely inappropriate. She's obviously been under a lot of stress with her grandfather. Don't believe a word she said—she's wrong about you, and you know it."

The thing is I DON'T know. Hannah could be completely right about me never passing those tests.

"I was just coming in to make a root beer float," my father says. "You want one?"

We both know his excuse is a total lie, but I gladly let my father steer the conversation away from Hannah. As he prepares the treats, I think about how glad I am not to be working with Hannah anymore— even if she wasn't the person who leaked Arctic Ninja.

HELP!

I wake up sweating from the most vivid nightmare I've ever had. The setting of my dream is similar to the snowy world of Arctic Ninja, but instead of being run down by evil toboggans and snowmen, I'm being attacked by large number 2 pencils falling from the sky. I run in a serpentine pattern to escape, which doesn't help because the pencils

serpentine

have a complex tracking system, and when I turn they do too. I scream for help but no one can hear me. I bolt out of bed and almost trip over Bodi sleeping on the floor.

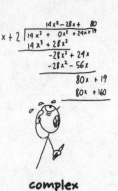

$$x + 2 \overline{\smash{\big)}\, 19x^3 + 0x^2 + 29x + 19}$$

complex

It takes several moments for me to calm down and throw on some clothes. After today's session there's only one more week of the focus group, and I'm already thinking about how much I'm going to miss it. But what I WON'T miss is having nightmares set in the icy world of Arctic Ninja.

At the Global Games snack table, Umberto almost knocks me over with his wheelchair. "Today is suggestion day—we get to give our own ideas for Arctic Ninja." He rattles off a million ideas he's been saving up. When Matt joins us, he's got

suggestion

improvement

ideas too. I, on the other hand, have been so worried about what Hannah said that I've barely thought of making an improvement to Arctic Ninja.

"Don't look now," Matt tells Umberto, "but here comes your hero."

Sure enough, when we turn around, Carly's walking toward us with none other than El Cid.

"We thought we'd hang with you guys today," Carly says. "Is that okay?"

Umberto stammers out a *yes*, and Matt races to clear a place at the table. I ask the gaming star if he's thought of any enhancements to the game. El Cid reaches into a pocket underneath his black cape and pulls out a piece of paper filled with a long list. Umberto cranes his neck to read it.

"Of course!" Umberto says. "The secret code should TOTALLY be in a different language than the rest of the game."

"Since the Eskimos have almost two hundred different words for snow, El Cid thought the secret code should have lots of different word choices too," Carly says.

"People who live in the Arctic may have a lot of different words for snow," I say, "but they have over a THOUSAND different words for reindeer."

When Umberto looks at me with surprise, I shrug and tell him I like watching animal shows.

Matt isn't even listening—he's telling a story about his uncle's trek

trek

to Alaska—but El Cid snaps to attention. He types into the note app on his phone and holds it up for me to read. Carly peeks over my shoulder to see it too.

"Well!" Carly says. "Looks like El Cid is impressed."

"I know lots of random information; unfortunately most of it is pretty useless." But that isn't to say I don't feel pretty great conversing with all these brainiacs today.

conversing

Tom calls us into the room and tells us the company really wants to hear any and all improvements to the game. We sit at our consoles and type in all the cool things we'd like to see in Arctic Ninja when it's released next year. After that, we break for lunch—a giant feast of sliders and mashed potatoes. I'm almost too full after the all-you-can-eat buffet to lift the controller off the desk.

I'm surprised when El Cid comes to join us for the afternoon session. He sits quietly between Carly and me, and when Tom blows his whistle for us to begin, El Cid gives me a thumbs-up.

Maybe it's because it's one of the last sessions, but the air in the room is full of more excitement than usual. Kids who are normally pretty quiet are whooping when their narwhal avoids a fatal harpoon or finds a missing part of the code. I'd always assumed El Cid got such high scores because he was fast, but sitting next to him now, I realize he seems relaxed and casual as he racks up more points than the rest of us combined.

Watching El Cid's score escalate gets me thinking about my own performance. I mean, is getting a high score on a video game THAT different from acing a state test? Don't they both require concentration? And who knew that relaxation was involved? I'm one of the most relaxed people I know—when I'm not taking a test, that is.

spellbound

I get so spellbound by this new concept that I don't realize my poor narwhal just got impaled by a giant icicle. As I start the level again, I look over at El Cid, who's just clocked an incredible 276,425 points. Whoever is underneath that helmet, he's an expert at getting to the next level in the game. For me, the next level is

impaled

passing and keeping up with the rest of my class. I may have just lost this level of Arctic Ninja, but I'm not willing to go back a level in real life.

I'm going to devise a way to unleash my gaming skills on the state tests.

devise

unleash

You Want Us
to What?

emergency

The next afternoon I decide to call an emergency meeting with my friends. Carly's cousin Amanda is in town for the weekend, so she tags along too.

"Watching El Cid gave me an idea for passing the state tests."

Amanda almost does a spit-take with her soda. Carly laughs and hands Amanda a napkin.

"I'll take any kind of help I can get," Amanda says. "What's your plan?"

"Believe it or not, acing Arctic Ninja uses a lot of the same skills as passing the state tests."

"I haven't seen any narwhals or killer snowmen on those tests, have you?" Umberto jokes.

"It's all about attitude," I explain. "I've been so focused on not failing that I haven't been having any fun."

attitude

This time it's Matt's turn for a spit-take. But unlike Amanda, he sprays a mouthful of root beer around the room. "Are you trying to say taking those tests can be fun? Because that would be insane."

"I'm not saying the tests are FUN," I explain. "I'm just saying we should play to our strengths."

Umberto and Matt look at me blankly.

"I think it's a good idea," Carly says. "Try to find a part of the test you can identify with—just like you draw stick figures to illustrate vocabulary words."

"But how can we have fun if we don't know what the topics are?" Amanda says. "You never know what you're getting when you open those booklets. I don't mind an essay on a cool topic like geology or reading your horoscope, but what if it's a subject I don't know anything about? How do I have fun with it then?"

geology

horoscope

Amanda's question is a good one, something I spent last night working on. (Yes, I did spend a Saturday night working—surprise, surprise.)

"Umberto, how fast can you create a phone app?"

"I can do a rough cut in maybe a few weeks."

"I can't believe you work so fast now," Matt tells Umberto. "That first app took you forever."

"Are you going to have Umberto animate your drawings?" Carly asks.

I tell her that's what I WAS going to do, but unfortunately it's too late. Time for Plan B. (Yes, I spent Saturday night making TWO plans.) I head to the hallway and holler upstairs. "Dad! Can you come down here a minute?"

My father joins us in the living room. He's a little disheveled, still wearing his sweats from cleaning the garage earlier. "You guys need something?"

disheveled

189 ★

"Yes," I answer. "We need someone who can help us make some storyboards. Fast."

A broad smile spreads across his face as if he's been waiting forever for someone to ask him just that.

My Own Kind of
Instruction
Manual

The idea is simple: figure out a way
to visualize the tests the same way
my stick figures help me visualize
vocabulary words. That's pretty
much what my dad does for the
movies. He draws panels for each
scene to help the director visualize
the movie before anyone even sets
up a camera. It would take me months
to do those kinds of drawings; lucky

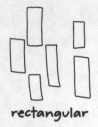

rectangular

for me, I live with a guy who—until recently—did that for a living.

My dad runs to his office and returns with his large rectangular pad and markers. Carly, of course, has come prepared with enough practice tests to keep the entire state of California busy for the next two years.

Matt, Umberto, Amanda, and I stare at Carly as she unpacks her bag.

"Who walks around with practice tests on a Sunday?" Matt finally asks. "You're a freak!"

"A freak who's bailing out a friend," she answers smugly.

I tell Matt to leave Carly alone. She's right—I need her help right now if my plan has any chance of working.

Carly hands me one of the essays to read, but I politely decline. Reading out loud is something I avoid at all costs. She realizes her mistake and starts to read the passage herself. Before Carly gets the first sentence out, my dad's already divided the page into several neat panels.

The essay's about the legend of Sasquatch, and Dad draws a series featuring the funniest, most original Bigfoot any of us have seen. My friends and I crowd around him, commenting on each panel as he creates it. He's having so much fun— the same way he enjoyed playing my video games but with a serious look in his eye that's comfortably familiar.

When Carly reads the questions at the end of the essay, my father

sasquatch

holds up the storyboard for us to see.

"What group of people have supposedly had the most sightings of Sasquatch?" Carly asks.

Umberto knows the answer but waits for me to respond. I point to one of the panels my father just drew of a man on a horse, chasing a herd of buffalo. "Native Americans?"

"Very good," Carly says in her best teacher voice. "Amanda, here's an easy one. The mythical Bigfoot is usually covered in what?"

mythical

Amanda traces my father's drawing with her finger. "Brown hairy fur?"

"Congratulations!" Carly says. "You two just passed the first essay on the practice test."

"Great, another fifty to go," I say.

My father looks up at me with a smile. "One picture at a time, Derek. Think you can do that?"

I look over at Carly, so happy in teacher mode, and at Amanda, so eager to find a strategy that will help her too. I need all the assistance I can get, and everyone in this room knows it. I'm going to pass these tests the same way I play video games—one screen, one image, one move at a time.

Dad turns the page in his pad, exposing a fresh sheet of paper. "Ready?" he asks.

And I am.

exposing

Drawings, Drawings Everywhere

frenzy

homophones

As much as Carly tries to organize all the pages from my dad's storyboard pad, the room still looks as if it's been hit by a hurricane. Dad's in a creative frenzy—drawing, crossing out, starting over—and the pages are flying. By the end of the afternoon, we've answered most of the test questions correctly. (Don't ask me again about homophones; I got that one wrong every time.)

Amanda collapses on the floor next to Bodi. "I can't believe I'm in L.A. for the weekend and we're studying!"

Carly tells her cousin she'll make up for it on her next visit by taking her to her favorite cemetery in Hollywood. The rest of us look at Carly as if she just burped in front of the pope.

cemetery

"We both love walking around graveyards and looking at all the tombstones," Carly says. "What's wrong with that?"

tombstones

She and Amanda stare us down until the three of us drop the subject.

Mom comes in with a giant bucket of fried chicken from Dinah's that sends Matt diving over the couch. When he realizes he almost knocked Umberto out of his wheelchair, Matt slows down and waits for everyone else to go first.

"Jeremy, I think this is some of your best work." Mom puts her arm around my dad and pulls him in tight. It dawns on me that they might start kissing in front of my friends, so I get ready to pretend I'm choking and need someone to give me the Heimlich maneuver. Thankfully, my dad just gives my mom a warm smile instead.

Amanda's face is buried in Bodi's fur; he looks as happy as a dog can possibly be. But Carly's still all business, gathering the storyboards into a giant pile while everyone else eats. I go over to help her, knowing she won't stop working on her own.

"If I can picture the essays in my head like a video game or comic book panel as I'm reading, maybe I can answer the questions as well as I did today," I tell her.

Carly looks around to make sure no one's watching, then leans over to give me a quick kiss on the cheek. "You're going to do great. I just know it!"

thunderstruck

I stand in the doorway, thunder-struck. Did that just happen? Or has doing schoolwork on a Sunday made me hallucinate?

I just got my first kiss!

What am I supposed to do NOW?

hallucinate

For the Win

spontaneous

Carly's quick kiss leaves me kooky for the rest of the weekend, which is probably good because it keeps me from worrying about school. I try to analyze what was going through her mind: Had she planned to kiss me? Or was it a spontaneous burst of support for my new study idea? Was I supposed to kiss her back? Is this something hanging in the air between us that I have to deal with now? I can only hope the answer to that last question is a resounding *NO*.

resounding

Of course I'd be lying if I didn't also say that part of me is a little thrilled by something so unexpected. A few months back when Carly was going out with that surfer Crash, I did feel a tiny bit jealous, but it's not like I've spent any time since then thinking about what it would be like to be her boyfriend. (A couple minutes, maybe, but not a lot.) As tempting as it is to dissect this new development, however, it's time to put on my game face and apply my storyboard study plan to these ghastly exams.

unexpected

ghastly

When I see Carly at her locker, all my crazy thoughts fly out the

nonchalance

window because she is totally, 100 percent normal and doesn't mention a thing about yesterday's peck on the cheek. I suppose that's good, but her nonchalance makes me wonder if I imagined the whole thing.

"I got a text from Amanda this morning," Carly says. "She's actually excited about the test today. I'm so glad she was in town for our brainstorming session."

"I'm not a visual learner like you," Umberto tells me. "But I still think the storyboard idea will be helpful."

Matt has on his good-luck Tony the Tiger T-shirt, which he always wears when he wants something to be GR-R-REAT! I don't know how great the tests will be; I'll be happy to pass by the skin of my teeth.

Principal Demetri isn't in to oversee the proceedings. Ms. McCoddle smiles and tells us to just do our best.

oversee

Carly turns in her seat to wish me good luck, but all I can think about is that kiss. I shake off the intruding thought and open my test booklet as soon as Ms. McCoddle gives the word.

intruding

The first essay is a letter to the editor complaining about a dangerous rotary on the highway. I imagine the illustrations my dad would draw if this were a movie, picturing cars stopping and going along the circular road. I answer three out of the four questions easily and guess at the one I don't know. So far, so good.

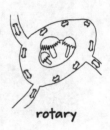

rotary

The next essay is about spotted

ocelot

acoustics

bongo

cats, including the cheetah, jaguar, leopard, and ocelot. I've watched a lot of animal shows, so this essay is okay too.

But the third essay throws me for a loop. It's about acoustics and has several technical terms. Since the subject is sound, I create an internal soundtrack to go alongside the images in my mind. I make good use of the millions of cartoons I've watched in my life by adding several CRASH! PING! BOOM! and AWHOOOOOGA! effects from my favorite Looney Tunes and Hanna-Barbera shorts. (Insert bongo sound of Fred Flintstone running here.)

"And...STOP!" I'm almost at the end of the test when I hear Ms. McCoddle's voice. She seems as excited as we are that today's test is finally over. "It's going to be a busy week—we have four more sections to do—but I think it's time to celebrate."

Ms. McCoddle brings out two plaid bags from behind her desk.

plaid

She reaches inside the first one and dramatically holds up a bundle of colorful Sharpies tied with thick ribbon. She hands it to Maria, who reads the attached card. "Thanks for being such a 'sharp' class." Maria helps Ms. McCoddle pass out the rainbow bundles.

dramatically

"If Ms. McCoddle was going to buy us presents at the 99 Cent store, she should've gotten food," Matt complains. "You wouldn't believe the bags of candy you can get for a dollar there."

"Are you kidding? I go through markers so fast, she can give me a new pack of these every day of the week," I tell him.

"I can't wait to talk to Amanda tonight and see how she did." Carly turns to face me. "So, what's the verdict?"

For a minute I think she's referring to yesterday's kiss but then realize she's talking about the test. "I don't want to jinx it, but I think I did okay."

jinx

The celebration continues with a surprise hot fudge sundae bar Mrs. Pankow has set up in the cafeteria to reward us for our hard work. I load up my bowl of ice cream with enough chocolate sauce to drown an eighteen-wheeler. Passing these tests is actually a possibility now. As I shovel the chocolatey goo into my mouth, all I can think about is how I can't wait to get home and thank my dad.

My Contribution

I use my new storyboard skills for the rest of the week, hoping I score enough right answers to pass. My storyboard theory's a little less helpful on the math test, but I try to visualize the word problems as comic panels too. By the end of the week, the whole school is loopy from all the testing, and we leave school on Friday as if it's the first day of summer vacation.

loopy

I stare at the TV for hours that night, barely paying attention to the comedies I've taped on the DVR. I don't think I've ever been so tired. My mom even lets me eat in front of the television, which is usually forbidden. I gratefully accept the plate of pasta and chicken without moving from my place on the couch.

The next morning is our last day of Arctic Ninja. I'm a little sad, but my father seems energetic when he drops me off, saying he's got lots of errands to keep him busy today. When I ask how the job hunt's going, he takes a few moments before answering.

energetic

"I actually started working on a new project this week," he says. "Something to keep me busy be- tween interviews."

I ask him what it is.

"You're not going to believe it," Dad says, "but I started working on a graphic novel."

I don't know why I'm surprised—my father certainly is creative—but I hadn't thought of him as an author before.

"I've never been the comic book or superhero type," Dad continues, "but maybe all the video games we've been playing have rubbed off. Not to mention how fun it was to do those storyboards with you and your friends."

I ask him what the graphic novel is about, and Dad seems embarrassed when he answers. "It's about this group of barbarians who turn into fish, creating this gigantic barbarian aquarium. It may sound corny but I'm enjoying it."

barbarians

I tell Dad I love the idea and ask if I can see what he has so far.

"Only if you help me draw some of the characters." My father seems more positive than he has in a while. He really is someone who needs to use his imagination to be happy. He tells me to have a good last day.

"Okay, everybody," Tom begins after we settle down. "We at Global Games want to thank you for all the great feedback you've given us on Arctic Ninja. We have a little something for each of you."

laden

Several interns magically appear, laden with gift bags bearing the Global Games logo. The shouts of joy from the other participants reach me before my gift bag does. When the intern finally hands me mine, I let out a whoop of my own.

The bag is overflowing with more video games than even Umberto owns. From Ni no Kuni to Me & My Katamari to Uncharted to Portal 2 to LEGO Marvel Super Heroes, it's stuffed with enough games to give any kid an embolism (I'm kidding, Mom!). A few kids complain that some of the more "mature" games aren't included but I'm not one of them.

Tom also tells us that we each will get a copy of Arctic Ninja when it finally hits the shelves next year.

cheat

"We can put together some cheat sheets and walk-throughs to sell online," Matt whispers. "Let other players know where all the Easter eggs are."

antique

I remind him how our plan to sell an antique doll online backfired,

backfired

costing me a lot of money. I hold up my bag of goodies and say this is good enough for me.

"We're also implementing several of your suggestions." Tom swipes across screens on his iPad. "We loved the suggestion of being able to change the Arctic blizzard to an Arctic lizard to an Arctic wizard. We think that'll add a nice dimension to the boss level part of the game."

The pogo guy lets out a shriek and ricochets around the room. I don't know what this kid's going to do with all that energy after the focus group ends.

"We also liked the idea of adding a catchphrase and thought *Chill out, you frozen nimrod!* was a good one. So look for that in the final version too."

"That's hilarious," I whisper. "I wish I'd thought of it."

Matt shakes himself out of a state of shock before answering. "That was MY idea."

"Get out!" I say. "Kids all over the world will be saying a line YOU thought up? No way!"

Matt pumps his fists in the air, so proud he might pop.

"How about impaling one last snowman before you go?" Tom asks.

The group responds with a giant YES!

evade

As I evade the razor-sharp icicles for the last time, I realize I've never had more fun at a console than playing Arctic Ninja. And when I look over at Matt, Umberto, and Carly, it seems as if they feel the same way too.

Before we break for lunch, Tom pulls me aside. "Derek, there's something I want to talk to you about." He flips through some drawings on his phone, which I realize are from my notebook. "Your dad texted me some illustrations you did of the Arctic Ninja characters. I love the narwhal wearing a sombrero—it's so random. Like a sponge living in a pineapple."

"That's what *I* said!"

"How'd you come up with it?"

I shrug and tell him I live in the world of random.

"I do too," Tom says. "So that's why I want your permission to add a sombrero to Skippy's final design. It'll be a great way for him to hide his tusk."

I MUST have misunderstood

what Tom just said. "You want to use MY narwhal in Arctic Ninja?"

"If it's okay with you," Tom says.

The thought of my narwhal design—WITH sombrero—appearing on millions of monitors across the country leaves me speechless.

speechless

"And in case you're interested, I'm running a weekend workshop in character design in Burbank next month. It's for high school kids, but I think you'd get a lot out of it."

When this focus group started, I felt like the stupidest kid on the planet. Today, I feel like I just might have something to contribute.

But there's one more thing I need to say to Tom before I score a seat in his workshop. "I'm really sorry about spilling the beans to my tutor.

It was nice of you to let me stay in the focus group."

Tom smiles and gives my arm a whack with the folded-up papers in his hand. "Your dad pulled for you on that one. He's a good man. But you already know that."

The thing is, I do.

Tom and I head to the cafeteria for one last mega-buffet. While I balance two pieces of corn bread on my plate, I notice Tom talking to Umberto. Does he want to use one of Umberto's designs too?

I sit next to Tom as he plays the pizza game app on Umberto's phone.

"You designed this yourself?" Tom asks.

Umberto tells him he took a programming class last year and has been designing basic apps ever since.

"Your apps aren't basic," Matt interrupts. "Show him the bowling game."

Umberto points to the icon on his phone and the familiar sounds and sights of a bowling ball knocking over pins fills the screen. Tom swipes his finger to hurl the ball into the pins.

overshoot

"The first few times you might overshoot," I tell him. "But you'll get the hang of it pretty fast."

When Tom scores a strike, he actually shouts.

"Umberto, would you be inter- ested in an internship this summer?" Tom asks. "I think you've got a lot of good ideas."

If it were possible for Umberto to jump out of his chair, he'd be bouncing off the ceiling right now.

"Absolutely!" Umberto answers. "I'd LOVE that."

Tom tells Umberto to make sure to leave his contact info so he can get in touch with his parents. When an intern comes to grab Tom, the three of us no longer have to control our excitement. In the midst of our celebration, I tell the others about Global Games using my narwhal design.

"With the sombrero?" Matt asks. "No way!"

"We are rock stars!" Umberto adds.

Umberto frantically texts his mom and brother while Matt and I gush over our friend's good fortune.

"This never would've happened if you hadn't invited us to this group," Umberto tells me. "I really need to thank your dad too."

I tell Umberto I didn't do anything, which is true. But his happiness is infectious, and I look across the cafeteria so we can share the good news with Carly. She's in line, stacking brownies onto a napkin.

infectious

"They're not all for me!" she exclaims. "El Cid's starving after racking up 346,000 points on that last game."

I don't know what's more alarming—the fact that someone scored that many points or the fact

alarming

that Carly's now enjoying El Cid's company in the private dining room. For a moment, my mind flashes to that quick kiss and I suddenly forget why I came over here. Luckily Carly jogs my memory.

"I saw Tom talking to Umberto. What's up?"

I fill her in on how Umberto will

be spending the summer at Global Games video camp. I also tell her about my narwhal and Tom's character design workshop. Carly congratulates me, then shoves the brownies into my hand before she goes over to congratulate Umberto.

El Cid must be hungrier than Carly thought, because he sneaks into the main cafeteria to find out what's taking so long. Carly tells our helmeted colleague about Umberto's good fortune. El Cid gives Umberto a long, sweeping bow like they're both members of King Arthur's court. Soon the whole table knows the news, then the room. It's a great way to end our time at Global Games.

I'm so busy taking in the celebration that I almost miss El Cid sneaking up beside me. He nods, then holds out his hand. I stare at him mutely until he points to the brownies. I pluck the first one from the top of the pile, pop the whole thing into my mouth, and hand him the rest.

pluck

I'm not quite sure, but I get the sense that El Cid just smiled underneath all that bulky headgear.

bulky

Hannah Rears
Her Head

In the weeks that follow, all my
friends and I talk about is how much
we miss the Global Games focus
group. It was great to play a part in
what will probably be next year's
hottest game. To fill the void, I
spend Saturday mornings with Frank
and Bodi watching old Westerns
on TV.

Mom sorts through mail at the

kitchen table, and Dad empties the dishwasher. He stands in front of the cabinet holding a stack of plates, frozen in his spot. "I'm not sure the sea horses work in here," he announces.

"You have my complete and total permission to paper over them," my mother says. She skims through a letter at the top of the pile. "Derek, remember Hannah? She wants a reference for her next job."

reference

"What?" I almost spill my bowl of Count Chocula, which gets Frank excited in his cage.

My father holds his finger to his mouth in a gesture for me to be quiet. I quickly realize he never told my mom about Hannah's tirade telling me what a loser I am.

tirade

Mom continues to study the

amnesia

letter, oblivious to the secret conversation Dad and I are having behind her back.

"Hannah must have amnesia," Mom says. "Did she forget how she didn't let us know when she was out of town for over a week?" She tosses the letter in the trash pile, and when her cell rings in the next room, she runs in to get it.

"I can't believe you didn't tell Mom about how mean Hannah was."

"Of COURSE I didn't," Dad says. "She would've dragged Hannah out of her dorm room to yell at her."

My father and I have seen my mom angry enough times to know he's only SLIGHTLY exaggerating.

fury

"She's one crazy mama lion," I say. "But Hannah might've deserved to sample some of Mom's fury."

"I didn't feel like bailing her out

of jail," Dad jokes. "Your mom, not Hannah."

He's only partly kidding.

"Hannah was wrong about you," my dad says. "Global Games is using your narwhal design. That's BIG! If I'm lucky, you can give me some fresh ideas for the barbarians in my graphic novel."

I appreciate the compliment, but both Dad and I know he'll probably never need my help in the art department.

"I didn't ask your permission to send those sketches to Tom," Dad says. "It turned out great, but I still should've asked."

I tell him I'm glad he DID send them. I also thank him for talking Tom into letting me stay in the group.

Mom finishes her phone call and

gets back to the large stack of mail. This time when she holds up an envelope, she's perfectly quiet.

"Is that . . . ?" I ask.

She nods and hands me the envelope. "The results of the state tests. Why don't you do the honors?"

"Are you kidding? I'm too nervous. YOU do it."

Mom calmly opens the envelope and hands me the letter without looking at it.

"Can't you just read it to me?"

deadpan

Her face is completely deadpan. "You are perfectly capable of reading this yourself."

Leave it to Mom to never let me off the hook when it comes to reading. I look over to Dad, who nods in agreement.

I take the letter and lower myself

onto the chair, nauseous and worried my chocolate breakfast might come back up. I scan through the letter until I finally get to the results.

nauseous

"I'm not in the lowest group!" The relief hits me like a rogue wave at the beach.

"I told you all that hard work would pay off," Mom says.

My dad pulls me in for a hug, and Mom joins in too until I collapse back on the chair in nervous exhaustion. I

exhaustion

feel as if I've been liberated from an evil curse that's lasted for months. I DID work hard, but not only that—I worked SMART this time too. After years of banging my head against an academic wall, it's finally sinking in that I'll always need to find my own best way to learn. I may not be the sharpest knife in the drawer

liberated

when it comes to most things, but there is one subject I'm the world's top expert in: ME. Figuring out a way to use my gaming skills to help me study WORKED. I guess coming up with new ways to master difficult tasks is what I'll be doing for the rest of my life.

But for right now?

I'm jumping on my board and skating over to Matt's.

Victory is mine!

GG

It turns out we all did okay, even Amanda. She's up from San Diego to go to a show at the Pantages with Carly this weekend, and they texted me this morning to come over for brunch.

The table's filled with bagels, three kinds of cream cheese, and a big pitcher of orange juice. Amanda can't stop talking about how my

coral

mosaic

abstract

developed

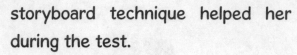

storyboard technique helped her during the test.

"There was a question about coral reefs, and I just kept picturing the fish from *Finding Nemo* while I was reading," Amanda says. "I'm sure I got every one of those questions right."

After we eat, Carly shows us the mosaic she's been working on in the spare bedroom. It's a large piece of wood with pieces of glass forming an abstract pattern.

The only art of Carly's I've seen are the pieces she's worked on in class; I had no idea she'd developed into such a good artist on her own.

"Can you make me one of those?" Amanda asks. "I'd love something like this for my room."

Carly tells her of course.

"Hey, how about some Rayman Legends?" Amanda asks.

No one has to ask me twice to play that video game—it's one of my favorites. I excuse myself to use Carly's bathroom as the girls head to the TV.

I check myself out in the mirror as I wash my hands. I'm so glad Matt isn't here to tease me for spending the afternoon with two girls. On my way back to the living room, I stop in Carly's spare room to take one more look at her mosaic. The glass is evenly cut and the whole piece is symmetrical. One thing you can say about Carly—she takes a lot of care with whatever she's working on.

symmetrical

Amanda must be staying in this room because there's a wheelie suitcase next to the bed and a pile of clothes on the floor. (It looks like Amanda's as messy as I am.) A vintage Donkey Kong T-shirt is on top of the pile. I know poking around other people's stuff isn't cool, but the Rubik's Cube on the nightstand calls my name. I'm turning the layers of squares, attempting to line them up when I spot a Trader Joe's shopping bag in the corner of the closet.

I drop the Rubik's Cube on the floor. What I THINK is sticking out of the bag cannot POSSIBLY be there. I tiptoe to the closet for a closer look.

Inside the bag are El Cid's cape, helmet, and gloves. Not a replica of his outfit, but the actual one.

WHAT IS GOING ON?

Carly and Amanda must hear me

and race into the room. "I can't believe you're such a snoop!" Carly shouts.

snoop

"I might be a snoop, but at least I'm not a liar. Is Amanda your cousin or not?" I then turn to Amanda. "Are YOU El Cid?"

Amanda closes the top of the Trader Joe's bag and shoves it deep into the closet.

"I WISH Amanda and I were cousins," Carly finally says. "We met a few months ago in the focus group."

"So that means..." I wait for Amanda to answer me.

rotates

She rotates the rows of the Rubik's Cube. "I don't know—am I?"

"Come on!" I yell. "This is important!"

Amanda finishes the cube in

record time and sits down on the bed. "This whole thing started because my brothers would never let me play their video games. I practiced a lot on my own so they'd play with me, then discovered it was something I was pretty good at."

"PRETTY good at?" I say. "You're the number one PlayStation gamer in the world!"

"I've got four brothers; I grew up pretty competitive."

Carly picks up the cube and scrambles the sides up again. "I told her that her brothers would be proud. It doesn't make sense to hide El Cid from them."

I'm always amazed at how people react to things differently. If I were the top gamer in the world, I'd make sure even the UPS guy knew.

"I keep telling Amanda she should admit to being El Cid—especially in a sport dominated by boys."

"People would be surprised, that's for sure." (I love that Carly just referred to playing video games as a sport.)

dominated

"I got into gaming to hang out with my brothers," Amanda says. "But discovered I liked having something that was just mine." She takes the El Cid gear out of the closet. "I'm such a fangirl, and creating El Cid was a cool way to have a secret identity."

"Matt and Umberto are not going to believe this," I say.

"Whoa, whoa!" Amanda says. "You can't tell them!"

"This is why I didn't say anything." Carly is now acting as if I'm not even in the room. She must be able to tell by my face that I'm upset because her expression grows softer.

"I HAD to keep it from you. If anyone in the focus group had found out, Amanda's cover would have been blown."

"I would NEVER blab!"

"Really?" Carly crosses her arms.

"What are you talking about?" I shout. "I can keep a secret! It turns out the things I told Hannah about Arctic Ninja weren't even part of the leak!"

It's only after the words have left my mouth that I realize I just let the cat out of the bag.

"You gave away Arctic Ninja secrets to your tutor?" Carly asks. "And you wonder why I didn't tell you about El Cid? You're one of my best friends, Derek, but let's face it, you're a blabbermouth."

I'm suddenly faced with a serious wall of truth. After spending all that time worried about Hannah being a big mouth, I guess I never really thought of myself as one too.

blabbermouth

"Okay, MAYBE I would've told Matt and Umberto about Amanda. And MAYBE they would've told a few other people."

"At least you admit it," Carly says.

I turn to Amanda. "But I don't understand why you're hiding! I'm with Carly on this. It's time for you to come clean."

Amanda tells us she'll think about it. I take the Rubik's Cube from Carly and she and Amanda watch as I struggle with it before finally giving up.

"I've got a few questions," I say. "Why does everyone think El Cid is a boy from Peru who goes to MIT?"

"Amanda WISHES she could get into MIT," Carly jokes.

"I've never even been to Peru," Amanda says. "Someone on the Internet started that rumor, and I let it spread. It sounds more exciting than a twelve-year-old girl from San Diego."

"Who surfs! We're going next weekend if you guys want to come." Carly the super-genius knows what I'm about to say and cuts me off at the knees. "But you have to promise not to tell Matt and Umberto. Okay?"

generous

I stare down Carly—the most generous and reliable friend I have. She's always bent over backward for me, so as juicy as this secret is, I guess I can agree. Besides, with my luck, if I DID tell someone it would be all over the Internet five minutes later.

"All right," I finally answer. "You can count on me."

I may not be the smartest kid in school, but I'm smart enough to know I don't want to mess with these two.

Amanda gives me a crooked smile. "I think a video game challenge is in order to seal the deal."

I turn to Carly. "It might be time to break out one of the retro games."

She rubs her hands together like a bad guy in a silent movie. "I'm thinking Ms. Pac-Man on the old Atari."

Matt and I never play Ms. Pac-Man but I'm definitely outnumbered

outnumbered

today. The funny thing is, I don't even mind.

As we head to the basement to find the old console, I ask Amanda a ton of questions. What's the highest score she's ever gotten on a game? (An incredible 527,988.) Did Tom know her real identity? (Yes, but he and Amanda's mother are the only people who do. Tom agreed to the private dining room to help her keep El Cid's identity secret.) Is her name really Amanda, or is that fake too? (It's Amanda. Duh!) What was her professional opinion of Arctic Ninja? (She thought the graphics were good but the game itself was a little slow!!!) Did any of her long list of improvements get picked? (The one about adding a real boss to the boss level.) I save the most important question for last.

"Did you let Carly and me win that competition?"

Amanda reaches into her pocket and pulls out a package of gum. She pops a piece into her mouth and tosses one to me. "I let Carly win," she says. "You just happened to be on her team. But the cod/code thing was all you guys; I didn't figure that out till later."

I should've known I never could've beaten a gamer like El Cid. Amanda must know what a letdown it is because she starts talking about how great it was that I helped her pass the state tests.

letdown

"Derek never gives himself enough credit," Carly says. "He's got a million great ideas."

"A million might be stretching it," I answer. "But I'm glad I could help."

Carly shoves a controller into my

obliterated

hand. "Ready to lose like you've never lost before?"

I point to Amanda. "But this time, no one lets anyone win, got it?"

"Then prepare to get obliterated," Amanda says.

I race back to the spare room and come out a few minutes later wearing El Cid's helmet, gloves, and cape. Both Amanda and Carly burst out laughing.

"I'm going to beat you BOTH," I say in my best Darth Vader voice.

"I don't think so." Amanda hits PLAY and makes her first move.

Let me say this: The helmet didn't help.

I got KILLED.

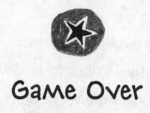

Game Over

My mother runs into the house to grab a sweater and is surprised to see my friends and me huddled around the kitchen table. I introduce her to Amanda, who she's never met before. Mom heads to the sink to wash her hands before shaking Amanda's.

After Mom goes back to her office, I open my laptop and turn the screen so we all can see it. "You sure you want to do this?" I ask Amanda.

Carly looks at her "cousin" expectantly. Umberto and Matt wait for Amanda's answer too.

Not revealing El Cid's identity to two of my best friends was one of the hardest things I've ever done in my life. But after seeing how disappointed Tom was with the Hannah leak—not to mention how much trouble I could've gotten into—I decided to actually try to learn something from one of my many mistakes. When Amanda finally decided to let the world know she was El Cid, she and Carly let me do the honors. The look on Matt's and Umberto's faces when I told them yesterday made it almost worth the wait.

Amanda finally lets out a sigh. "I've been putting this off for long enough. Let's do it. My brothers are going to have a conniption!"

conniption

"Or maybe they'll love you even more," Carly says.

Leave it to Carly to always focus on the bright side.

Amanda's finger pauses over the keyboard.

"Come on!" Umberto says. "The world wants to know the true identity of El Cid!"

Amanda looks a little sad. "I kind of enjoyed having a secret. It'll be different now."

"Yeah," Matt says. "Everyone will know that girls kick butt!"

"You don't have to do this now," Carly says. "Do you want to take a few days and think about it?"

A slow grin spreads across Amanda's face. "It's like jumping into the ocean without your wet suit. There's only one way to do it." She looks at Carly, who grins right back.

"One, two, three, GO!" Without a moment's hesitation, Amanda hits ENTER on the laptop, sending out a photo of herself sitting in front of my PlayStation with a score of over 220,000, holding El Cid's helmet.

fallout

The fallout happens over the next few hours. First a Japanese gaming site is plastered with Amanda's picture. Then the Sony chat rooms start spreading the news. Amanda's phone pings with new texts. Throughout the afternoon, Umberto goes from site to site, calling out various responses. (It's the most fun he's had in years.)

"This one blog says you're the fangirl of all fangirls. Another one says you're a champion of kid power." Umberto continues to scroll. "I bet you have a ton of interview requests by the end of the day."

champion

"And a dozen new challenges for El Cid." Amanda holds out her phone so we can see the texts filling her screen. "These are just from my brothers."

Carly reads the texts and laughs. "I TOLD you they'd be proud."

wallop

"Yeah, if they don't wallop me first—in a game, that is."

I microwave a few bags of popcorn for us to enjoy while we help Amanda get through this hectic afternoon.

hectic

"We're friends with El Cid!" Matt whispers to me. "Would it be lame to take notes next time we play her?"

"I don't know if it's lame, but it certainly doesn't sound like fun." I hand him a bowl of popcorn to pass to the others.

When I go into the den to find the laptop's power cord, Carly follows me in.

"Amanda's life is about to get insane," Carly says. "But it'll be exciting too."

sponsor

"She could even get a sponsor out of this." I act like the idea is mine but that kind of thinking is totally Matt's.

I find the computer cord hiding under my dad's sweatshirt. I look at Carly standing beside me near the bookcase. Amanda showed a lot of courage today; now it's my turn. I reach over and give Carly a quick kiss on the cheek. She seems as flustered as I was on the day she kissed me.

"Um...I'm glad you found the cord," Carly stammers.

"I know—I hate it when my laptop loses power."

"I freak out when the battery power goes below fifteen percent," Carly says.

"Me too! I always worry I'll lose what I'm working on."

Carly and I are officially having the lamest conversation in the history of the world. But then as we head back to the kitchen, she grabs my hand. Is she trying to hold hands or help me carry the power cord? I'm not sure! I feel stupid and thrilled at the same time. Amanda may have given up her secret identity today, but now I'M the one with a secret. My mind races, wondering if my friends at the table will be able to tell there's just been an earth-shattering shift in the person formerly known as Derek Fallon.

earth-shattering

tailspin

As I'm about to head into a mental tailspin, Matt shouts at me from across the room. *"Chill out, you frozen nimrod!"*

It's actually a pretty good piece of advice.

GOFISH

JANET TASHJIAN

How would you finish the line "My life as _____"?
A rewriter. Like most writers, I spend more time rewriting than writing!

Are you more of a reluctant reader like Derek, or are you a big reader?
I'm a massive reader. I've been reading at least three books a week for most of my life. I can't imagine a life without books.

If you could be any living person, who would you be and why?
I'd love to be my son, Jake, for a day to see the world through his eyes. He's got such a great, original view of the world— I'm sure it would be fascinating.

You've traveled around the world. Where would you say your favorite place is?
Where I live. I love Los Angeles. I love the comedy, the music, the restaurants, the beaches, the museums, the mountains, the people. And the weather. I REALLY love the weather.

How did you come up with the My Life series?

Jake used to love books when he was young, but as books became more challenging, reading became difficult. Because he is a visual leaner, he started drawing his vocabulary words on index cards with markers to help in his learning process. When friends would see them, they'd always laugh at how funny and creative the drawings were. At the same time, I was doing school visits all around the country, listening to teachers, students, and librarians talk about reaching reluctant readers. I wrote *My Life as a Book* for Jake and other kids like him.

If you could be any cartoon character, which one would you be and why?

I mean, who DOESN'T want to be Bugs Bunny? He's unflappable, sarcastic, and has the best comebacks. Bugs totally holds up, even eighty years after he was created.

What's your favorite word Jake has ever illustrated?

It would have to be the word "colleague" from the first book in the series. He drew two guys in prison uniforms on a chain gang, shackled to each other. Brilliant. It still makes me laugh.

Who is your favorite book character and why?

That's an almost impossible question to answer! I love Joey Pigza, I love Arnie the Doughnut, and I love Einstein the Class Hamster. Yes, the last one is one of mine, but he does have a special place in my heart. I'm a sucker for wisecracking characters.

What kind of books do you like to read?

I spend so much time in the fictional world when I'm writing that I end up reading a lot of nonfiction to balance it out. But

I also keep up on what my friends are writing, as well as the latest adult fiction. I have a huge collection of vintage children's books, too.

Do you base your characters on people you know?
Sometimes I'll steal a habit or quirk from one of my friends, but never a whole character. It's much more fun to make up characters from scratch.

What is your favorite thing about writing the My Life series?
There are so many things I love about the My Life series, but first and foremost, the greatest part is getting to work with my son. When students ask about our process, I tell them I write the book first, then go through it to highlight age-appropriate vocabulary words, as well as words that would be funny for Jake to illustrate. Then he takes over, drawing more than 220 illustrations for each book in the series. His illustrations literally make me laugh out loud. I love watching him work; he's such a perfectionist and so professional. He's done more than a thousand drawings for this series!

I also like the fact that the books are read by kids all around the world in so many different languages. It's exciting that "reluctant" readers have embraced Derek, his friends, and their crazy adventures. Getting to tell Derek's story is an absolute joy. I find it funny when people talk about what a "bad" kid he is and how he always misbehaves—I know so many boys just like him, and they aren't bad at all!

Are you a fan of cartoons? Do you have a favorite cartoonist? Who and why?
I am a GIANT cartoon nerd. I'm a big fan of watching Saturday morning cartoons—even if it isn't Saturday. We have a

cartoon collection that goes all the way back to the 1930s. I love print cartoons, too. Jake and I read *Calvin and Hobbes* in chronological order; it's my favorite comic strip of all time and the reason I dedicated *My Life as a Book* to Bill Watterson. I read every cartoon in *The New Yorker*; Jake reads every *Garfield*. He has a daily cartoon app on his phone so he can keep up with his favorites. I can't imagine a world without cartoons, so it's great to have a cartoonist in the family.

What did you want to be when you grew up?
Students ask me this all the time, and I wish I had a better answer. When I was young, I was too busy playing, reading, and studying to think about career goals. I envy people who knew what they wanted to be by age ten. I was not one of them.

When did you realize you wanted to be a writer?
Before Jake was born I traveled around the world, and when I got back to the States, I had to fill in some forms. One asked for my occupation and I put down "writer," even though I'd never done anything more than dabble. But deep down, I always felt being a writer would be the greatest job in the world. It took me several years after that to make that dream a reality.

What's your first childhood memory?
I remember cooking candies in a little pan on a toy stove that I got for Christmas. I was maybe three. I'm not sure if I remember it or if I just saw the photograph so often that I think I do.

What's your most embarrassing childhood memory?
I was singing and dancing in a school assembly with my first grade class when my shoe fell off. I kept going without the shoe, hopping around the stage—the show must go on.

What was your worst subject in school?
I always did well in school, but for some reason I forgot all my math skills and now can barely multiply. I'd love to know where all my math skills went.

What was your first job?
I've had dozens of jobs since I was sixteen—working on assembly lines, babysitting, washing dishes, waiting tables, delivering dental molds and telephone books, selling copy machines, working in a fabric store, painting houses. . . . I could fill a whole page with how many jobs I've had.

How did you celebrate publishing your first book?
By inviting my tenth-grade English teacher to my first book signing. The photo of the two of us from that day sits on my writing desk.

Where do you write your books?
Usually in my office on my treadmill desk. But because I often write in longhand, I end up writing everywhere—on the beach, in a coffee shop, wherever I am.

When you finish a book, who reads it first?
Always my editor, Christy Ottaviano. We've been doing books together for almost two decades; I consider her one of my closest friends.

How do you usually feel once you've completed a manuscript? Are you ever sad when a book you are writing is over?
Relieved! I don't really miss my characters; they're always with me.

Are you a morning person or a night owl?
I like waking up early and getting right to work. I'm too fried by the end of the day to get anything substantial done.

What's your idea of the best meal ever?
Something healthy and fresh, with lots of friends sitting around and talking. Definitely a chocolate dessert.

Which do you like better, cats or dogs?
I love dogs and have always had one. I'm allergic to cats, so I stay away from them. They don't seem as fun as dogs, anyway.

What do you value most in your friends?
Dependability and a sense of humor. All my friends are pretty funny.

Where do you go for peace and quiet?
I head to the woods. I'm there all the time. I love the beach, too.

What makes you laugh out loud?
My son. He's by far the funniest person I know.

What are you most afraid of?
I worry about all the normal mom things, like war, drunk drivers, and strange illnesses with no cures. I'm also afraid our culture is so invested in technology that we're veering away from basic things like nature. I worry about the implications down the road.

What time of the year do you like the best?
The summer, absolutely. I hate the cold.

If you were stranded on a desert island, who would you want for company?
My family.

If you could travel in time, where would you go?
To the future, to see how badly we've messed things up.

What's the best advice you have ever received about writing?
To do it as a daily practice, like running or meditation.

How do you react when you receive criticism?
My sales background and MFA workshops have left me with a very tough skin. If the feedback makes the book better, bring it on.

What do you want readers to remember about your books?
I want them to remember the characters as if they were old friends.

What would you do if you ever stopped writing?
Try to live my life without finding stories everywhere. For a job, I'd do some kind of design—anything from renovating houses to creating fabric.

What do you like best about yourself?
I'm not afraid to work.

What is your worst habit?
I hate to exercise.

What do you consider to be your greatest accomplishment?
How great my son is.

What do you wish you could do better?
Write a perfect first draft.

What is your idea of fun?
Seeing comedy or music in a tiny club.

Is there anything you'd like to confess?
I love dark chocolate.

What would your friends say if we asked them about you?
She acts like a fifteen-year-old boy.

What's on your list of things to do right now?
EXERCISE!

What do you think about when you're bored?
Story ideas.

How do you spend a rainy day?
Watching comedy.

Can you share a little-known fact about yourself?
I love to make collages.

He's a ninja in training, but can he
find out who's vandalizing the
school with mysterious graffiti?

Keep reading for an excerpt.

The Dojo

Mom runs her veterinary practice from the office adjacent to our house, so that means there's always lots of people and their pets coming up and down the driveway. As Dad gets ready to drive Matt, Carly, and me to the martial arts studio, we're stopped by a woman walking a ferret on a leash.

The ferret wears a top hat and a tutu of colorful feathers. The poor

adjacent

ferret

plumage

animal looks like a Muppet with pink plumage.

"Please say Dr. Fallon can help Zippy with his stage fright. He's performing tonight and he's a wreck!" The woman coos and whispers to the ferret, who seems like he'd rather be anywhere else.

Dad assures her Mom has experience with lots of different animals and shows the woman to the office.

"You should totally get Frank a top hat," Matt says. "But definitely not a tutu."

"Frank needs a Lakers T-shirt," Carly says. "He watches more basketball on TV than I do."

My family and I are the foster home for Frank until he's old enough to go to Monkey College to learn to help people with physical disabilities do things like open doors, turn on lights, and fetch water bottles. Lately he's turned into a giant sports fan too, watching TV alongside me and my dog, Bodi.

fetch

I wanted Frank to wear one of those foam fingers they sell at games, but Mom was afraid he'd eat it. I fought her like crazy but she put her foot down. I guess it's a good thing she did because when I went to find the finger under my bed, Frank had already chewed it to a stub. Luckily he was okay; I on the other hand received yet another lecture on responsibility.

stub

We finally pile in the car and head to the martial arts studio. Because Carly wanted us to join the other studio in Santa Monica, she complains for a bit until we hit the highway. Umberto called the studio yesterday to see if they could accommodate him in a wheelchair but they said there would be a lot of kicking and mat work in class and he'd be better off studying with the instructor one-on-one. It's a shame because Umberto's the funniest kid I know and he'd be hilarious to have in class. Umberto said he didn't mind, but I wonder if that's true.

On the drive over, Carly talks about directing the play and Matt shoots me an I-Told-You-So face. We pretend to listen until Dad pulls into the parking lot of the dojo. He gets lots of texts at his new job—even on weekends—so he returns phone calls outside while the three of us go in.

The first person we see is a

twenty-something guy wearing a black gi who introduces himself as Dave. I try not to stare—the guy is lean and mean with a shaved head and pierced eyebrows. He might be the scariest guy I've ever seen in real life, so I'm surprised when his voice is quiet and I can barely hear him.

gi

pierced

"Welcome to the Way of the Thunder Shadow," he says. "A place where discipline and action unite."

The studio is dimly lit with black folding chairs in the waiting room. The walls are painted black with one wall of mirrors. Everything is black or red, except for the small fern withering in a pot by the door.

withering

"Do you have an appointment with Sensei Takai?" Dave asks.

I tell him we do and that we're interested in their Junior Ninja classes.

Dave slowly bows. "Sensei Takai will be with you soon."

The three of us sit in the darkened room and wait for what seems like an eternity. (Turns out, it was only about five minutes.)

erect

An old man with the most erect posture I've ever seen enters the room quietly; Carly jumps out of her chair when she realizes he's standing beside her.

We wait for the sensei to speak but he just looks at us and smiles. After a few awkward minutes, I

blurt

blurt out why we're here. "We want to be ninjas and we heard you're a great sensei."

The old man continues to stare

and smile while the three of us fidget.

The sensei wears a shinobi shozoku and head scarf covering everything except his eyes, and canvas tabi boots with split toes and rubber soles. All of his clothing is black. He looks like every ninja in every movie I've ever seen except he's old and standing perfectly still. We follow his lead and try to sit quietly.

Almost ten minutes later, he clears his throat to speak. His voice is even quieter than Dave's, so the three of us have to lean in to hear him.

"Welcome to my dojo," he says with a bow.

We made a list of several questions we wanted to ask but now the three of us just take turns looking at one another, not sure what to do next.

"Today's lesson is over," Sensei Takai says. "You practice until next time."

"Practice what?" Carly asks.

Sensei Takai smiles, then waves his hand to dismiss us.

dismiss

"But what are we supposed to do?" Carly asks again.

He bows one more time and leaves the room.

Carly spends most of her time trying to get everything just right, so an assignment with no instructions is unacceptable.

unacceptable

"It's obvious what we're supposed to do," Matt says when we're outside. "Right, Derek?"

I smirk like of course I know, but

I have absolutely no idea. Carly calls my bluff immediately.

bluff

"You guys are as clueless as I am, so stop pretending you're not!"

Matt and I finally admit we don't know what Sensei Takai expects us to practice.

"I didn't think being a ninja was going to be so complicated," Matt says. "I thought we could just act like spies."

I spot my dad at the coffee shop across the street. He waves and points to his phone, indicating he's almost finished with his call.

"The question is, are we coming back next week?" I ask my friends.

Carly shakes her head. "I hate not knowing what's expected of me."

"Welcome to my world," I say.

trickery

On the way home, Dad lets us stop for burgers and fries. Over our meal, we tell him about the session with Sensei Takai.

"Aren't ninjas trained in trickery?" Dad asks. "Maybe Sensei Takai is not telling you what to practice on purpose."

Matt, Carly, and I exchange glances. Have we just been tricked by a ninja?

A School Mystery

When we get to school on Monday, Mr. Demetri calls an emergency assembly. As we file in, the principal paces across the stage, impatiently waiting for us to take our seats. When he finally gets to the podium, he doesn't look happy.

impatiently

"There was an act of vandalism at the school this weekend. And you KNOW how I feel about vandalism."

podium

spree

Minotaur

tolerate

justice

He doesn't need to remind us how he reacts to destruction of school property. Last year some kids from the high school broke several windows on a crime spree and Mr. Demetri didn't rest until they were caught.

Mr. Demetri motions to Ms. Mateo, the assistant principal, and a slide fills the screen behind him. It's an illustration of a demented Minotaur that looks like it's spray-painted on the back of the school. A few kids start to laugh at the odd-looking creature but one look at our principal's face shuts them up fast.

"I will not tolerate this," Mr. Demetri continues. "Whoever is responsible will be brought to justice, mark my words."

Ms. Mateo gets up and makes a few announcements about the school play, mentioning there's a sign-up sheet outside the cafeteria. Carly beams when her name is mentioned as the director.

As we head back to class, Umberto skids his wheelchair, blocking our path. "You know what this whole vandalism thing means, don't you?"

"It means Mr. Demetri's going to want someone's head on a platter," Matt says.

But I know what Umberto's thinking because I'm thinking the same thing. "It means our school needs a hero."

"It means our school needs a spy," Matt says.

"I'm not sure I like where this is going," Carly says.

Matt, Umberto, and I say the next line in unison: "It means our school needs a NINJA!"

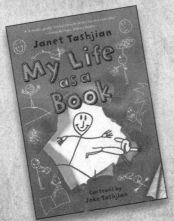
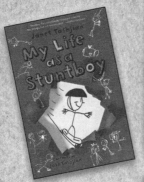